IT WAS BROAD DAYLIGHT in fashionable Beverly Hills when Jim Foraker came upon the still-warm body of the most beautiful girl he had ever seen. She had been brutally murdered. The police lost no time in pinning the killing on Jim himself.

Here was a spot that made Jim's combat experiences in the Pacific look simple in comparison. He knew if he didn't find the fiendish killer, he would go up for this himself.

"Refreshingly direct in the telling, here is a story which avoids irrelevant clues and unnecessary characters. Each person is important in the unfolding of events . . ."
—Brooklyn *Eagle*

Gordon McDonell knows how to write a suspense story. He's sold over a dozen stories to the movies and did the screen treatment of "Shadow of a Doubt" and "They Won't Believe Me." *My Sister, Goodnight* has been bought by Franchot Tone.

THE CHARACTERS IN ORDER OF THEIR APPEARANCE

Major James Foraker . . . A combat hero in the Marines. Handsome, intense, he acted on impulse. He didn't know that chivalry is dead.

Letitia Lane . . . Talented young actress whose personal life reached a tragic crisis.

Lieutenant Ives . . . Plain-clothes man. A nice guy—for a cop.

Wilson . . . Another plain-clothes man. Ives' "help."

Elsa Marble . . . A sensitive gal. She was interested in only three things—her husband, her baby, and Jim Foraker.

Tom Marble . . . Elsa's husband and Jim's best friend. A successful movie director.

Janet Holbrook . . . Letitia's twin sister—and just as lovely.

Begg Holbrook . . . Janet's husband.

George Sellick . . . Erratic young author, moody and aloof. Formerly in the Marines with Tom and Jim.

The moon on the one hand,
The dawn on the other:
The moon is my sister,
The dawn is my brother.
The moon on my left
And the dawn on my right.
My brother, good morning:
My sister, good night.

—HILAIRE BELLOC

My Sister, Goodnight

by GORDON McDONELL

WILDSIDE PRESS

Printing History
Published in *Blue Book* Magazine, October, 1947
Little, Brown Edition Published January, 1948
1st Printing......November, 1947
2nd Printing........March, 1948
Montreal *Standard* condensed version Published 1948
Newark *Sunday News* condensed version Published 1948
Bantam Edition Published July, 1950
1st Printing........June, 1950

Chapter One

I FOUND HER just about halfway up Coldwater Canyon Alley, lying against the wire fence under those eucalyptus trees. She had on a fuchsia red sweater and an expensive tweed skirt that was rumpled up high over her knees and her legs were perfect, nylons and a pair of brogues with big tongues. She had a necklace of those deep brown polished cowries that men like myself bring home from the Pacific and that dark burnished hair of hers was slid part way across her face. She couldn't have put her lipstick on more than an hour or so ago—it was deep and quite unsmeared, and the mouth still had a composed half-smile as though she had just drawn four aces. Twenty-two, -three, -four, something like that.

I stopped the car and got out and went over and felt her pulse although I had a hunch it was no good. I've seen so many in the last few years, there's a feel to them directly you see them, the way they lie and a feeling you get. Her wrist was still warm though, she couldn't have been dead more than a few minutes. I must have been the first person to happen along. For a moment I wondered what to do and I pulled her skirt down properly. I thought of all I had read in ridiculous books that have nothing to do with real life; leave everything alone and look around for clues and stuff like that, above all don't touch or make extra tracks or marks anywhere. Report at once. Then I looked at her face again and after a moment I just picked her up as gently as I could and put her in the back of my car. I did look around for clues too even after that, but there wasn't anything and as for tracks the ground was quite hard and I wasn't the one for that game anyway. Then I got in and drove straight on up the alley to the junction with Coldwater Canyon Road and turned left down to Beverly Hills again. I had the sedan

1

and nobody took any notice. I had the strangest feeling all the way to the station. I felt that if anyone had stopped me and tried anything I would have knocked him cold.

I hit the green light at Santa Monica, so I didn't have to draw up alongside any other automobiles and when I reached the station there was a parking spot almost right outside. It was reserved for police cars only but the other places were too far. Her head had fallen sideways again and I put my hand gently against it and straightened it and her hair tingled against my hand. I could still feel it tingling on my palm as I went up the steps and into the station and I wondered how long hair stayed with that electricity in it after a girl was dead and I thought that maybe there was still about a newly dead person an aura of their souls too if there was still the electricity. You never can tell.

The desk sergeant was on the telephone as I came in, something about a dog. I leaned on the desk and looked at him, the usual type of desk sergeant that looked as though he might have been sent right over from a studio casting director, he was so typical. He put the phone down with his eyes on mine and then he wrote something on a pad and rang a bell and a cop came in. When the cop went with the paper the desk sergeant looked at me again and said, "Well, Major, what can I do for you?"

I said, "There's a girl in my car. She's dead. You'd better send someone down to take her out, someone responsible."

He looked at me closely.

"You mean a girl just died in your car, Major?" I never have liked policemen and I never have liked desks. I said, "No, I don't mean she just died in my car. She just died in Coldwater Canyon Alley from a rabbit punch. I found her there ten minutes ago so I brought her right in. She was still warm when I got her and no one else has seen her yet."

"You mean you found a stiff and moved it, eh?"

"Certainly I did. You'd better send—"

"Send a man to get her," he cut in. "Since you know so much of what we should do, Major, perhaps you also know

2

you've broken the law and even marines aren't immune from that." He rang a bell. "Why did you move her?" he asked me while he was waiting for the cop.

"Because I didn't want anyone else to find her. I can tell you just how she was and where, give you the exact picture."

His eyes were on my ribbons. He said slowly, "You know, Major, a man with your record ought to know better than to act the way you did. You're pretty young for a major, aren't you?"

The cop came in, and the sergeant said, "The major here has brought in a dead body he says he found in Coldwater Canyon Alley." He thought of something and turned to me again. "Was it north or south of the fire station?"

"It was south," I said. "About a hundred yards south."

The desk sergeant gave a resigned sigh and turned back to the cop again. "I guess that's us then. Only a hundred yards further and it would have been one for West Los Angeles. It's in his car outside he says. Go down and get what identification you can." He looked at me again. "Did she have a purse?"

I nodded and he turned back to the cop again. "Okay, get going then and find out what you can without touching her—it's a girl he says."

The cop looked at me and then he nodded.

"Yeah, you bet it's a girl. If it had been some old trout he'd never—"

I started for him. My hands were beginning to shake a bit as they do nowadays after the Pacific. The desk sergeant said, "Take it easy, Major." I stopped myself just in time. The cop stood his ground but he didn't like it. I could have given him around twenty pounds. He waited till I stopped and then he said, "Okay, Sergeant, I'll be going," and turned on his heel and went.

The sergeant picked up the telephone and dialed a number. He seemed to have forgotten all about me but I knew he hadn't. I was all the time trying to figure out how such a girl could have gotten herself into a mess like that. I

3

thought to myself it must have been some guy back from the war because of those cowrie shells. Probably the usual story of the girl's having changed her mind while he was away. I felt a strange feeling, as though of jealousy, and I couldn't figure that one, since I haven't had too much of an opinion of women since the war started. But she seemed different. She couldn't have been like that. I wondered who the guy was and again I felt that feeling directly I thought of him. That any man should have known her that well. After all, you've got to know someone darn well to want to kill him.

The desk sergeant was talking on the telephone to the receiving station next door, and he told the doctor to come over right away to examine her. He put the phone down and pressed a buzzer and called in someone named Ives. Then he spoke into his transmitter, calling cars number twelve and sixty-one to proceed at once to Coldwater Canyon Alley and seal it and look out for anything pending arrival of the detectives.

Ives came in with another man. They were both plain-clothes men and I could see I would have to try not to let them make me feel all caged up. Once I get to feeling caged up then there's always trouble ahead. A lot of people think it's the flying that does it but it isn't the flying. I've been like that ever since I was a kid, long before I ever put a finger on a plane, long before the war. But it pays to let people think it's the flying, especially people like Ives. If they knew it was just surplus electricity, if they knew it was genuine all-the-year-round stuff, then it makes me out something else. And that's no good, giving them something to pick on. I was thinking about how to control it when they came in and I was watching Ives's face for clues. The other man was his help, you could see that at once, you could see he wouldn't originate trouble.

The desk sergeant sketched it for Ives. Ives listened. Ives was still just listening when the cop came back up the steps

4

with her purse. He put it on the desk and said that was all, she had no rings, but she had a shell necklace like sailors and marines bring back from the Pacific, and he looked at me as he said it. Ives picked up the purse and started through it. The cop said it looked like her neck was broken but the doctor was examining her right now and would make his report shortly. Ives listened all the time while he went through the purse. The cop said she sure was not hard to look at and the sergeant said that was all thank you and I dug my hands in my pockets as the cop went out.

Ives was looking at me. He looked for about ten seconds and the help looked too and then Ives said, "This way, Major," and the help went ahead along a passage. I followed him with Ives right behind me. They took me into a plain, small room with the walls only part way up to the ceiling. There was a bare desk and some chairs. Ives sat down behind the desk and told me to sit opposite while the other man stood in the shadows behind me. Ives zipped up her purse that he was still carrying and put it down.

He said, "What did Letitia mean to you?"

"Is that her name—Letitia?"

"Didn't you know?"

"I never set eyes on her before."

I was thinking, Letitia, that's a corny kind of a name for her, disappointing somehow.

Ives said, "Then why didn't you leave her where she was and call the police from the nearest telephone?"

"I should have. I just didn't. I've no explanation."

"Hm," Ives said. He tapped a soft little tattoo on the desk with fingertips of his left hand. "Let me see your identification."

I took out my wallet and handed it to him complete. He took out my driver's license, and studied it, and checked my eyes and hair.

"What is your name?" he asked me.

"James Quentin Foraker."

5

"Date of birth?"

"October thirtieth, nineteen fifteen. You needn't worry, it's my wallet all right."

He looked through my other papers and handed me back the wallet, and got up, nodding to the help. "Let's go."

We went out through the front hall. The doctor was standing by the desk talking with the sergeant who was on the telephone. The sergeant was evidently talking to the coroner who was telling him to call Pierce Brothers—I heard something about Pierce Brothers as we came through the hall. The sergeant handed the telephone back to the doctor and he said yes, it was a fractured cervical vertebra. He listened some more, then said all right and put the telephone down. He told the sergeant that it was not really necessary to hold an autopsy as the cause of death was quite obvious, but that as a matter of routine and to make everything aboveboard it was as well to have Pierce Brothers perform one. The sergeant said okay, he would tell them and turned to Ives and asked who she was. Ives handed him her purse and told him he was taking me up to the alley right now and would see him later. The sergeant said okay and we went out to Ives's car.

They asked where my car was first and went to take a look at her. She was still sitting in the same position as before as though nobody had disturbed her. I got that feeling again as I saw her once more, sitting there in my car like that; it was a curious sensation.

I turned away and waited for them by their car. I didn't want to be with them while they said anything about her. It wasn't that I expected them to make cracks like that cop, but I just didn't want to be with them while they said anything about her. The ambulance came for her just as they had done looking, and Ives gave the men the go-ahead. The next place she would be going was Pierce Brothers. I knew that about her too. Gradually I would know more and more about her, maybe.

Ives shot me a quick look as they came up and then

6

opened the door and nodded. I got in with him in the back while the help drove. I could see that I was in for more questioning and I was glad it wasn't far to the alley where I could stretch my legs and get uncaged for a little time. It went through my mind, as Ives began his questions, that I had taken no exercise at all since ten o'clock that morning and it was now four in the afternoon. I would have to get some more in before sunset or else there would be trouble in the night, especially if they were going to keep me in some office with klieg lights. It was clear that my wisest course was to try and answer as politely as possible and hope they would release me before the night.

Ives said, "You told the desk sergeant she died of a rabbit punch. How did you know?"

"In my profession," I said, "one gets to know that kind of thing."

"What are you doing in Los Angeles, Major?"

"I'm on leave."

"When did you arrive and where from?"

"I arrived a week ago from San Diego where I docked two weeks ago."

"From the Pacific?"

"Yes."

"Tell me where you're staying and for how long and where you are going next."

"I'm staying with friends at 6441 Rodeo Drive, Beverly Hills. I shall be here another three weeks. Then I go to Quantico, Virginia, where I'm going to be an instructor in combat flying."

"How long is it since your last leave?"

"Just over a year."

"Where is your home?"

"New York."

"Are you married or single?"

"Single."

"Are your parents living?"

"Yes."

7

"And you're not going home for any of your leave?"

"I shall probably go for a few days before taking up my new appointment."

"Who are these friends of yours here?"

"Captain and Mrs. Marble. He was my best friend in the Marines. He's out now and back at his studio where he works as a motion picture director."

"You don't see very much of him then in the daytime?"

"Of course not."

"But you see Mrs. Marble no doubt?"

"No doubt. When she isn't busy with the baby which is most of the time."

"You must have plenty of time on your hands."

"More than I had in the Pacific, for a change."

"Why did you go up Coldwater Canyon Alley just now?"

"I was on my way to the hills to take some exercise. I need a great deal of exercise. I took the alley because it looked interesting. I did not have the girl with me. I did not murder her in the alley or anywhere else. I had never seen her before in my life."

We had reached the alley. A patrol car was standing by. The help stopped to let Ives speak to the cops. I got out and started walking up the alley. I was getting my hands in a bad state of shakes with all the damfool questions and I was goddamned if I would sit in that automobile any longer. I heard the help shout after me but I didn't give a damn and kept right on walking. I was interested to see if he would start shooting but he didn't. He drove the car after me. I still kept right on walking after I heard him right behind me and he had to slow down to five miles an hour which was the pace I was walking. I guess he looked kind of stupid and I began to feel a bit better. When I got to the place where she had been, I stopped and he stopped too, and got out and came up to me and started to get tough. But he wasn't too good at it. Ives would have been ten times better. I just cut through it and told him that was where she was lying when I first saw her. He was interested at once, besides seeing in it a way of recovering his dignity. He started asking me questions about how she was lying, exactly where, whether I noticed anything else anywhere around, any people, any dogs even, anything at all. I told him just how it had all been. He was good at this kind of thing, quick and smart, and my respect for him grew from the former low. His name was Wilson and he had been through the mill, you could see that. He had quick brown eyes that took everything in with an all-embracing steady brown stare that yet had a light behind it that saved it from being literal. They weren't as smart as Ives's eyes, but they were all right.

Behind the wire fence against which she had been lying was a concrete tennis court belonging to the house which backed onto it. Although the road was called an alley and was an alley in the sense that it went past the backs of the houses on Beverly Drive and was used for garbage collection and garden refuse and so on, yet it was really a country lane and a very beautiful one too, while on the other side of it there were green hills and trees and a general well-kept, parklike yet country appearance, something like parts of Connecticut, if you substituted elm for eucalyptus. Wilson took in the whole picture, noting even the empty garbage cans still lying outside the backs of most of the houses, and asking me if they had been just the same way when I came through. I told him that as far as I could tell there was no difference.

Ives joined us and Wilson reported to him what I had told him. Ives said that the whole neighborhood was being canvassed by men he had just assigned and everything around there was being taken care of and the sooner they got on to the girl's home the better. He turned to me and said that I would not be wanted any further at present but that I was to remain on call and asked me the number of the Marbles' telephone. I gave it to him and asked him if I could not accompany them. He looked at me a little curiously, as he had done several times before, and asked me why I should want to do that. I said that it was simply that

9

I was exceedingly interested in seeing the matter to its conclusion since I had been in at the start of it. He said that he was unable to let me do this and would get in touch with me later on. He dropped me off by a patrol car that was going back to the station where I had left my car. Then he and Wilson drove off to the home of Letitia. I did not even know where that might be.

Chapter Two

WHEN I got back to Rodeo Drive I found Elsa upstairs bathing the baby. Tom had not come back from the studio yet. The little upstairs nursery smelled of talcum powder and the room had in its warmth and intimate gaiety, with its little frescoed animals on the walls and general cleanliness, the air of being very consciously the kernel of the house. It struck me as I came in that you could see very definitely, especially now when it was snugly lit against the gathering dusk at the close of the day, that the room was the heart of things and knew it and was proud of it, with the baby kicking happily and splashing Elsa's sensitive, sensible face. In her eyes as she turned to me when I came in there was such a look of deep serenity that it made me feel quieter, but I think she noticed at once that all was not well with Foraker. Elsa was always quick in the uptake.

I sat down on the edge of the bed as she went on with the child's tub and asked me if I had had a good hike. I did not wish to trouble Elsa with what had happened. I knew that she would have to be told soon because of the police calling up later on and perhaps causing anxiety with possible inquiries about me and so forth, but I wanted it to come to her from Tom and so I said that the hike was fine and asked if Tom was going to be late or not. She said he had just called to say he would be working late tonight. She finished the powdering and pinning and zipping up and gave him

10

his bottle and turned the lights low and put a hand on my shoulder and said, "For a man who's been hiking you're still mighty charged up, Foraker. Come and let's have a martini."

It was no use trying to conceal things from Elsa, I might have known that. I laughed. "And get charged up some more?" I asked her.

"Maybe you will and maybe you won't," she said, "but you look like you could do with one just the same."

Over the drinks downstairs I told her what had happened. It was not easy to know how to begin. As we were sitting there in that ordinary, familiar living room, just down from the putting of a child to bed, with Elsa's common sense permeating everywhere, it did not seem anything other than utterly fantastic, the thing that had just happened. It was no wonder that I was a little tense, trying to start telling her about it. But somehow, drawn out by Elsa's stillness as she sat on a low stool, calmly holding her drink, not pressing me with a single question, I told her the whole thing as simply as I could.

She took it with greater composure than I had expected, and yet, looking back on it afterwards, I suppose I should have known that she would take it in the way she did. You couldn't faze a woman like Elsa, with her solid New England stock. I've known Elsa for around two years or so, and that's a lifetime in these days. I met her the same time Tom did, at a dance in San Diego when Tom and I were on a leave together. I remember telling him then that he was hooked and by the right person too if there could ever be such a thing, and he had laughed and said that coming from me that was the best testimonial any woman could have.

So now, when I had finished and was waiting for her to say something, she got up quietly and started pouring the other half of our martinis. She handed me my glass and sat down again and smoothed her skirt down over her knees and then she said, "You know, Foraker, you're really an Elizabethan character. You don't belong in this century, but we can do with lots of Elizabethans in this century I think."

I said, "Just exactly what are you stalling about, Elsa?" but even then I think I knew something of what she meant, because once before, one evening when we were all just a little high in San Diego, the night Tom and she had gotten engaged, she had said something about my being Elizabethan in connection with some stuff she was talking about gallantry. I forget now just exactly what it was all about, something to do with a girl in the hotel they were kidding me about, but Elsa had come out with that remark about my being Elizabethan, and now it looked as though she had forgotten she had ever said it before, or at any rate that she thought it bore repetition.

She said, "You know just what I mean. If you hadn't been you, you'd never have moved the girl at all. Then you wouldn't be in trouble."

"Who said I was in trouble? Ives is much too level-headed a guy to think I'm responsible, or at any rate to come to any unproved conclusions. He'll soon find whoever did it."

"I suppose so," she agreed. "But all the same it was a corny, romantic act, and you're a dope to live as you do."

"You just said you could do with lots of people like me."

"Certainly I can. But you don't do yourself any good by refusing to grow up."

I asked her what she meant—why was moving a girl not being grown up, why wasn't it just a decent normal thing to do, a simple example of respect for the dead? She said that it was all of that, but it was also chivalrous, and chivalry was adolescent. I didn't say anything, I was beginning to get the shakes again and I realized that I still hadn't taken my exercise. Even Elsa was beginning to coop me up and that was something that she didn't do as a rule. One of the reasons I can stand being with her is that she doesn't fret at one like most women. But now she was starting to fret at me and I didn't like it. I finished my martini as quickly as I decently could, but even so I couldn't get out of the room before she

12

had really started something. She said, "Foraker, why won't you try and tell me what's the matter? You know I don't make a habit of butting in, but it's high time I did for once. Is it something about not going home, dear?"

I said, "What do you mean, not going home?"

She gave me a quick glance.

"Tom told me," she said after a moment, "why you didn't care to go home."

I put down my empty glass and got up. I said, "Tom had no business—"

She interrupted me as I was on my way to the door. She put a hand on my arm and got right in my path and looked up at me with that sane frankness of hers and said, "Now, listen, Foraker dear, I simply will not permit this. You're going to sit right down again and behave yourself. Damn it all, you're so busy with your own feelings you haven't given a thought to mine."

I stared at her. "What do you mean," I asked her, "just how do your feelings come into it?"

"Well, it doesn't do my inferiority complex any good to be unable to help you, does it?"

Somehow with Elsa she always would find a way to break the tension in me, even if only for a little while. I could not help a smile and sat down again beside her on the sofa and said, "Actually, it's nothing serious, my not going home you know, Elsa. It's simply, as I told Tom, that Mother is always trying to marry me off every time I come back and I never can put a foot in the house without finding some babe who has been sicked onto me with strictly honorable intentions. I know why Mum does it—she's always hated my flying. She's always wanted me to settle down, but she just doesn't seem to realize that it would be much smarter on her part to let me pick my own wife. The way she behaves has the reverse effect and makes me want to stay single the rest of my life."

"I see," Elsa said slowly, "you mean you want to get married?"

13

"Why not? It's quite normal isn't it?"

"Quite. But," she went on calmly, "it just doesn't happen to be true in your case I don't believe."

I didn't know what to say for a moment. I couldn't see this attack, I didn't like it. I said, "That's good, Elsa. That's the first time I've been told that. Everyone else has always said I want to stay single."

She nodded. "I know," she said. "I know that perfectly well, and you've always said in rebuttal that you want to get married but can't find the right girl, I'll bet."

"That's just it. They are thrust upon me. Maybe they might be the right ones if I found them for myself."

She smiled a little.

"Foraker, you're not trying to tell me that you never can find a girl, are you?"

"Oh, I know, sure I find plenty of girls, but they aren't the ones to marry, the ones you just pick up on leave."

"It's been done," she said. She got up and walked over to the window. Outside the moonlight was already beginning and you could see the palm trees over on the next street. She drew the curtains across the window and came back to the little settee by the fire. She said, "You know, baby, you're just frightened of responsibility, that's what's wrong with you. So you'll invent any excuse not to get hooked."

I don't know why she said that, what it was that brought such a statement from her. It almost looked as though she was deliberately trying to get me all charged up again worse than ever. Elsa was a kind, considerate and tactful person with plenty of social adroitness, and it was clearly not a matter of mere gaucheness on her part. I said, "It looks to me as though you've decided to try the great modern panacea and use me as a psychological guinea pig. Why don't you have me lie down on the couch and you sit at my head and take notes? Certainly I'm normally afraid of added responsibilities, but they're not the reason I haven't married. I just don't happen to have fallen in love, that's all. The simplest reason is often the true one, you know."

14

It was at that point in our conversation that it happened, the odd sensation came over me. I felt it coming over me as I was speaking those last words, the corniest, oldest sensation in the world that you get first when you're a kid caught at the jam or telling a lie. Or telling a lie.

It was those words that gave it to me, "I just don't happen to have fallen in love," and they kept on going through my head, the sound of them, nagging at me and kind of jeering at me and I felt that Elsa was looking at me in a similar kind of way and I got the feeling of being all charged up again and I got up to my feet once again as Elsa was saying, "Okay, honey, so you've never fallen in love."

I said, "Just what do you mean, Elsa?" and I could see she heard the tension in my voice because her face went a bit white. But then she set her jaw in that defiant way she had when she knew that there was something she ought to do, something that was unpleasant and hurtful but had to be done, like firing a maid or cutting out a thorn or having to wait for Tom, and she said, "I've already told you what I meant. I said you'll invent any excuse not to get hooked, and now, this afternoon, you've just invented the best excuse of the lot. It's so good, Foraker, that it's unbeatable, because in this particular case there's not the remotest chance of getting hooked, is there?"

I walked out of the house. I simply walked right past her and out of the house. I walked up the street, I walked on and on and on up the street, and then when I got to Sunset I caught a taxi that was going by empty. I told the driver to go up in the hills. He asked me where in the hills, and I said I didn't give a damn just as long as it was up, high up, where there was room to breathe. He looked at my uniform and shrugged and said, "Anything you say, Major."

I don't know just where he did go now, I simply didn't notice the directions he took, but when we were way up somewhere along Mulholland I stopped him at the foot of a firebreak and gave him his fare. There was plenty of moonlight to see by and the track led away up to the very top, and I went on up and up climbing steadily all the time with the lights in the valley spread below me on one side, while the lights from the coastal plain became visible on the other, and when I was at the top I could see the whole of the hub of the western world spread out before me, and I thought to myself that down there, somewhere among those lights, anonymous and discreet, was the killer of Letitia.

Chapter Three

I WAS determined to find him. As I stood there on the top of the hill beside the water tower which was built on the high point, I wondered to myself why I was determined to find him, what it could possibly matter to me who killed that girl, a girl whom I had never met. I walked around the tower to keep warm, for there was a strong night breeze blowing from the big mountains on the far side of the inland valley and I did not have my leather flight jacket with me as I should have had. I walked around and around the tower, looking again and again at the views upon all sides, the myriads of lights, the sharp contours of the treeless California hills, and, far off, the emptiness beyond the lights which I knew to be the ocean. Owing to the inland breeze there was no coastal fog and you could see right as far as the ocean's rim where the lights of the cities ceased along the beaches.

I began to feel a calming of my blood, that same balm of spirit that can come from flight. Although still chained to the ground, at least I was high up, looking over part of its expanse. I began to feel able to rationalize my feelings and to think coherently about the things which Elsa had said. What she had said about my wishing to evade responsibility of marriage might be true. It might be. But if it were true, then according to what little I had gathered about psychol-

16

ogy, there was somewhere tucked away in my past the key to the reason for my fearing responsibility. But the trouble with those things was that they were always too pat, too oversimplified, as though you could account for man's life by his impression of one incident in his childhood. Too much importance could easily be placed upon that one incident and too little upon the kind of physical person that he is. Surely the physical chemistry of a person is the key to that person's mental and spiritual processes, surely people do not take this enough into account when so glibly talking about psychology. At any rate, the physical and psychological sides must be reciprocal, and a lot of people, like Elsa in this case, don't seem to take that into account. Elsa had no business to take liberties with me like that. I should have taken her up on it instead of bounding out of the house like a child. I should have told her that it had not seemed to occur to her that a person with an abnormal amount of physical energy had to lead a very different kind of life from most; that to inflict my scatty form of living upon a girl was not fair to the average kind of girl; that it was not at all easy to find the girl who would or could stand for a man who would be continually off on different forms of adventure necessary to his physical well-being. If I suddenly wanted to breeze off in the middle of the night on a hike or a boat or a few hours' night-flying, then there was no more reason why she should expect me not to than for me to expect her to come with me. A fine marriage that would be, a coming and a going all the time. Better to stay single than to contract the wrong kind of marriage. If that was showing lack of responsibility Elsa had her words the wrong way round. The truth was that I had more than an average sense of responsibility or I would obviously have been married and divorced long ago.

The night wind was getting colder, but still I did not leave the water tower's vantage point. Something kept me gazing at the lights below, gazing out at the night and the sea of the night sky. There was a distinct glow in the sky

17

over the cities, but farther off over the big mountains it was darker and more natural, lit only by the light of the moon and stars. As I looked at this piece of the sky that was clearer and unimpeded by man I saw against it in my mind's eye, as it were in ghostly and enormous silhouette, the image of Letitia's face. I saw every line and contour of that face, so well had I memorized it that afternoon, and it seemed as though I had known her all my life—it seemed as though I knew just exactly how she would speak and how she would move about, and for a brief instant, just then as I looked up into that night sky, I even knew the sound of her laughter in my ears. Only the color of her eyes was wanting to me. I could not see the color of her eyes, for her eyes were closed, and she seemed to be laughing to me in her sleep.

Soon the vision faded and I turned away, walking down the hill again towards the firebreak. And all the way as I walked down the firebreak to the road, and all the way along the road on my way back to a more crowded place where I could get a ride, all the way I could feel a lightness in my spirit which was strangely combined with a feeling of much sorrow....

When I returned to Elsa it was quite late, and I found her reading quietly alone in the living room. She looked up to me as I came in and examined my face in her knowing way. I said that I was sorry for having walked out on her when she was alone. She said that my dinner was ready for me and came to sit with me while I ate. She had kept everything prepared for me as though she had known that I would return.

I looked across the table at her as she sat so still in the candlelight and I said, "You know, Elsa, I truly did fall in love this afternoon. I don't profess to understand, but—it's there."

She put her hand over the table between us and touched my arm.

"It's happened before," she said. "I've heard of it happening—I don't just mean in classical literature either, I've read of it in modern life.

"I never did, but then I don't read. How does it turn out?"

She said, "Well, it can be rough. But that depends on the person, Foraker. Maybe with you—" She let her words fall to a little silence.

"Maybe."

I was thinking that there was little to expect, and I think she was thinking it too because she had had sense enough not to just shrug it off. She got up and busied herself with pouring me some coffee from the little percolator on the side table.

"There's been some telephoning while you were out," she said. "First, Ives called to speak to Tom, so I gave him the studio number. He asked me if you were staying here so I said you were. Then Tom called just now to say Ives had been to see him."

"I expect he was checking up on me."

"Yes. Poor Tom seemed a bit upset. It seems he knew her."

"He knew her?"

"She used to play bit parts for him sometimes."

I thought to myself what a strange thing it was that Tom had known her. It seemed strange also to think of Letitia as having acted. I had somehow never pictured that. She had looked to be very much superior to that kind of thing. I've never had much time for actresses, at least not for motion picture actresses. But Tom wouldn't have known her except professionally. He would only have known her very slightly as a director, probably knew nothing about her personal life at all. For that I would have to go elsewhere, I felt sure.

"Did he say anything else about her?" I asked Elsa.

"No," she said. "He said he wanted to talk to you, and I told him you were out. He seemed worried because you'd told Ives you would be on call and I got the idea that Ives is wanting to see you again. I told Tom I knew you would be back shortly, and he said he would be too."

I wondered what was worrying Tom, but I didn't think too much about it. Tom was like that always, even when he was my wing man, the wartime Tom. He was always worrying about his instruments which was partly the reason why he was such a brilliant flyer. But when he came in I saw at once that something must be pretty wrong.

I suppose I know Tom better than anyone else does except perhaps for Elsa, and even there I've certainly known him longer and under circumstances of danger and stress that she would never have seen him in, and directly he came through the door I could sense there was something —there was a certain way he had with his shoulders, I can't ever describe it but I know it so well. And, too, he couldn't disguise his relief at seeing me there. I couldn't understand it and asked him what Ives had said.

He said, "He wants to see you in about a half-hour." He turned to Elsa and said, "Would you mind?" and she looked a little surprised but left the room at once. Tom waited till she had closed the door behind her and then he said, "Tell me something, Foraker, had you ever met Letitia before?"

I was beginning to get impatient. There have often been times when old Tom would make me feel a bit impatient with him and this was certainly one of them. I said, "Of course not, Tom. What exactly has got into you this time?"

He looked at me still bewildered.

"But then why on earth did you move her when you found her?"

That was something I wasn't going to go into with Tom. I felt let down too, if that was all he had been worrying about. I mean when I say let down, I felt annoyed at his making so much of it all. I said, "I moved her because I felt like moving her, I guess. You know me, I never do the orthodox thing. It's in character, isn't it, you dope?"

20

He nodded in a reluctant yet pleased way and said, "Yes, that fits the Foraker mercury all right. I must say I'm mighty glad to hear it too, because I've had a bad hour with Ives, I can tell you."

I said, "I wish to high heaven you would tell me."

He took his pipe out of his pocket and sat down and said, "Take it easy, Foraker. You don't have to go for twenty minutes and this will take all of that."

I sat down and tried waiting—I knew it was the only thing I could do anyway. Tom was not trying to be deliberate. He just never could help it. He always had to start everything at the beginning. He had such a deep sense of chronology, or else a sheer inability to hit the high lights and let the rest go, that he always used to annoy us over his flight reports—I mean his unofficial flight reports. When you asked Tom what had happened after something he had been on, when he would come back with those things in his plane which meant he should not have returned at all, he would climb out and start right in, "When we took off it was, as you may recall, clear, with cloud at three thousand at ninety degrees. We proceeded for thirty-five minutes on a two-seventy-degree course at three hundred speed during which time nothing occurred and I had time to—" and then he'd not only go into all that he did with his instruments but all that he thought and felt about this and that, both personal things and otherwise.

I believe that he had to go through this routine or he would have been quite unable to recapture the things which did matter later on. Because it always seemed as if those high lights which were the only matters of importance to anyone else were of no more importance to Tom than any one of the many other things that went to make the total picture of his day. You would have thought that a man like that would never make a good fighter pilot, yet/he certainly was, and one of the best. I think that the same process could be speeded up in his brain to an infinite degree, so that he never lost the continuity of

21

combat for a fraction of a second, whereas with most people it was more a matter of intuition. Perhaps if you break intuition down it is just that—a sense of logic speeded up to an infinite degree. Perhaps that was also why Tom was a good motion picture director, because he would think the picture right through, frame by frame, in perfect continuity. Anyway, that was what he did now. He told me the story of his acquaintanceship with Letitia just like that, frame by frame, as it were.

He started on the day he first met her, how he had been passing on some bit players, and she was one of them, and he had just spoken a couple of words with her, how her work was at first a little awkward, how she had improved fast, not needing to be told anything more than once, as though it came naturally to her, which he had found such a pleasant relief after so many trying tussles he had had in the past with stupid bit players—and not only bit players at that, he took time out to assure me. For a moment I thought he might be going into a dissertation on the stupidity of certain motion picture stars, but his sense of continuity preserved him from that and the next point he came to was that Letitia had somehow impressed him, almost without his realizing it, to the extent that in nearly every one of his pictures after that first one about a couple of years ago, he had found himself automatically looking for a part for her when reading through the script before casting it.

And so she had played her little parts in each of his pictures. Not, he assured me, because of anything personal— I knew, he said, his feelings for Elsa and how he was a perfectly contented married man—and neither because he built parts in especially for her, but simply because she was competent and had a catholic quality which enabled her to fit varying types of roles so that whatever the story there was in every case a part for her, however small.

During all this time he had never spoken to her except in his professional capacity when directing her, until on one occasion he had approached her during an intermission and

22

had had a short talk with her about her work in general, which by then had quite impressed him, and he had suggested to her that she might try to be tested for a quite big role in a picture about to be made at another studio in a part which he considered would suit her admirably. She had told him then that she did not wish to do this because she had no ambition to step higher—she had no need of it financially, and all that she wanted was to play occasional bit parts just as she had been doing up till then.

The idea of someone's working for him as a hobby had somewhat annoyed him—he admitted it quite frankly—and for a while his interest in the girl had gone, what slight professional interest that there was, but then later on he had found himself watching her at work and wondering why it was that she should be motivated to do it at all if she neither needed the money nor wished to progress. It occurred to him that there had always been something strange about her, the way in which she always dwelt within herself, and now that he thought about it thus, it did indeed seem almost as though there were something in her soul of inner tragedy, that she might perhaps be doing her acting so that it in turn would act upon her as an anodyne for whatever might be troubling her.

Finding himself embarked upon such romantic speculation he had promptly taken himself in hand and dismissed the matter from his mind as being overfanciful. But then, not long after he had done this, he discovered a new development which made him believe that perhaps his notion had not been so fanciful after all. For it was about then that her sense of tragedy deepened and became almost obvious, confirming what he had previously supposed, but now, instead of driving her to sink herself more than ever into her work she must evidently have reached some form of spiritual limit, for her work began to be adversely affected until it soon became so bad that he knew that she would have to be replaced.

He was conscious of the fact that he disliked very much

23

the idea of letting her go without a word as is so often done in such cases, for not only was he fond of the girl but he also felt sorry for her and, too, by now he felt quite convinced that there was some tragedy lying behind the whole thing which was causing her life to go wrong. However, he would probably have done nothing more about the matter and let her go in the usual way had it not been for the fact that on that last evening, which was three nights ago, he had been driving out of the studio gates and had passed her as she was also on her way out.

He decided on the spur of the moment he would offer her a lift and use the opportunity to do whatever he could to help her. He stopped the car and asked her if she would care for a ride home. She accepted politely and it turned out that she too lived in Beverly Hills, at an address as good as his own, if not better. It seemed that she used to have an apartment in a fashionable building but that then the building had changed hands and the new owner had dispossessed her to occupy the flat himself, and for the past few weeks Letitia had been staying with her family while looking around for another apartment. For a moment Tom had wondered whether this could have anything to do with her upset, but he soon found that it had not—that whatever was upsetting Letitia was, as he had supposed, some matter of far greater depth and emotional importance than the loss of an apartment.

For after she had told him of her apartment troubles and the ice had thus to a certain extent been broken, even though on a somewhat superficial plane, Tom said that he was then emboldened to ask her straight out what was the matter, saying that it had been quite obvious to him that she was under a great strain and that he felt very badly about the way her work had been affected.

And then, quite unexpectedly, he had found, upon getting no answer from her and turning to look at her as she sat beside him in the car, that she was in tears, sitting there crying silently to herself in the corner.

24

For a moment he had wondered what to do next, and then he had decided to stop the car at a convenient place under the trees alongside the avenue and wait for her to speak. He did this, and she made no comment upon his stopping. She was trying her best, he could see, to cease the flow of those silent tears. After a while she succeeded in doing this, and as he waited patiently for her to speak, she began to do so.

She told him that she was at one of those crises in the life of a human being when no one except that being can decide his fate, one of those supreme and fortunately rare moments in a lifetime when the oneness and the aloneness of a human are brought sharply home. Those, Tom said, were of course not her exact words which he himself was unable to remember precisely, but that was their purport, and he had recognized at once that he was in the presence of something too big for him.

When she continued, and said that in order to solve her tangled web she had decided to marry a man whom she did not love, and that it was the imminence of this marriage which was causing the extra strain, then at that point Tom had, as he put it, waded in, and he had begged her not to go through with such a marriage, adding that whatever her problem might be, such a step not only was not a solution but could only make matters far worse than ever before.

At first she demurred strongly against refusing to go through with her plan. She said that she had promised him and that she could not go back on her word, that if she did he would take it very hard indeed for he was very much in love with her, although they had only known each other for about a week.

At that Tom had said she had no business to think along those lines, to weigh her life's happiness in the scale against a man's week-old love affair, something which could not constitute a life's happiness. For even a woman could get over a week-old love affair and a man most certainly could.

Letitia said nothing for a while to that, and Tom could

25

not be sure whether she was weighing what he had said about the man, or whether she was thinking of the effect of a refusal upon her own life, how it would affect her other problem which the marriage was supposed to solve. At length she said that it was impossible for her to come to a decision that night, but she would sleep on the whole matter and then decide what she would do. She had then thanked him very much for his kindness and sympathy, which she said had been of great value to her in her time of trouble. She was by now quite calm again and, seeing she had regained her composure, Tom had driven her home to her family's house and that was the last he had ever seen of her.

In the intervening time between that and the news of her death he had often wondered what decision she had come to. He had always had a feeling which she had left with him as one of his parting impressions from her, that she would in the end follow his advice, and now with the news of her death he felt convinced that she had done just that and been murdered for it. This was why he had been so upset, coming on top of the added shock of finding that I, his house guest, had brought Letitia in.

He had of course told Ives the whole story, and Ives had naturally questioned him very closely about me, asking whether he had introduced Letitia to me and so on, and the facts that she had only met the man at about the same time that I had arrived in town and that he had given her a necklace such as a marine like myself might well give to a girl, had all very naturally served to increase Ives's questions, for it had to be admitted that the coincidence of it all was very strong. Ives, in fact, had been quite skeptical of Tom's saying he had not introduced me to her, and the only reason he had not sent for me right away was that first he wished to check up with Letitia's family to try and find out what had been her problem. You could not, he finished, really blame Ives for feeling like that about me, especially in view of my having picked the girl up.

26

As Tom finished talking I could see by the way he spoke and the little shake of his head that he was still worried about me and the trouble I was in by my own folly, but I was not interested in Tom's feelings just then. I was thinking to myself over all that he had told me about Letitia. I was seeing that scene in the car under the trees alongside the darkening avenue, and I was thinking to myself that it was a strange fate that the gods dealt out in their cards, that it should have been Tom who had been sitting there and comforting Letitia and that it should not have been me.

And I was thinking to myself that it had been, in a way, so nearly me, the way that I was now so intermingled in her affairs, and I knew that it was I who had to carry them on from there, I and not Tom, Tom was out of it. Tom was married to Elsa anyway—his only real interest in Letitia was the fact that he felt partially responsible for her death. It was not in any sense to be compared with my interest in her, it was not to be compared with that at all.

I was thinking these things to myself as I got up from my chair and walked across the room to the door and thanked Tom for telling me his story and told him not to worry about me with Ives, that my safety was not really in the least at stake, that he must not blame himself over Letitia because he had done the right thing. He had said to her just the words that I would have said to her myself if I had been there with her that evening instead of him.

I told Tom good night and said that it might be quite late when I returned from seeing Ives and I thought to myself, as I closed the door behind me and left the house, that I had very many things to find out from Ives and that it would take a great portion of the night.

Chapter Four

IVES was not there when I reached the station, but Wilson arrived shortly after I did. He looked at me in

27

his straight-faced way and said, "Glad you're here, Major. Let's go, shall we?"

"Go where?"

He just gave a little nod as though I'd told him the time or something. He had already started out the door and I had to follow him. When we were in the car he said, "Lieutenant Ives is waiting for us at the house."

I said, "Have you found out much yet?"

He looked at me and back at the road again.

"Quite a bit, Major, quite a bit."

I didn't care for his tone very much but I ignored it.

"Did you find out why she was going to marry that fellow?"

He looked at me again.

"So you knew about that too, did you?"

"Captain Marble told me."

"Captain Marble told you."

I said, "What are you getting at, Wilson?"

He swung the car off the boulevard up one of the Beverly Hills avenues, I couldn't see which one. He said, "I mean you're very interested in a girl you never saw before, that's what I mean."

I saw it was no use talking to Wilson any more so I quit. Evidently I was still under a cloud, or a new cloud had just come up. I had a hunch that I wouldn't be long finding out what it was all about and my hunch proved to be right. Wilson stopped the car outside one of the houses on the avenue and we went in. Wilson rang the front doorbell and after a moment a maid come and opened the door. Wilson didn't say anything. He just walked in and the maid stepped aside and I followed Wilson. He walked down a short entrance hall and turned in to a big living room. Ives was sitting at the other end of the big room. He was sitting with a girl. The girl was wearing a black dress. I didn't look at her face until I got close because I was looking at Ives's face to try and get a clue, but it was more poker face than Wilson's could ever hope to be, so when I got close I

28

looked at the girl's face and I stopped dead in my tracks and my heart turned right over. It was she.

"Letitia," I said.

It was Letitia. There couldn't be any doubt about it. It was the girl I had picked up dead. I felt my hands beginning to shake a little and I clenched my fists. Ives had turned and was looking at her in silent inquiry and she shook her head, but without taking her eyes off me.

"I don't think so," she said to Ives. "I'm pretty sure that wasn't the voice."

Ives, said, "Tell him the exact words you heard. Major, you repeat what she says."

There was a pause. Her eyes were on mine and my eyes were on hers. They were blue, they were deep, deep blue. I was thinking to myself, she was dead, there hadn't been any doubt, so it couldn't be she. There was only one answer. There couldn't be two girls like that unless they were twins, there couldn't be two Letitias in the world unless she had a twin sister. It must be her twin sister—that's what it must be.

Ives's voice came over my thoughts.

"Tell him the words you heard," he repeated.

She was still looking at me and her face was very white and she had been crying. I waited for the words and I thought, it hit you hard, twin sister, it certainly hit you hard.

The words came. The words came very low, but they were clear. They were clear and like bells—each word was like a low clear bell.

"Good night for now, darling," she said.

I repeated the words after her, I kept my voice steady and repeated them and we were still looking at each other.

"Good night for now, darling," I said.

After a moment her eyes dropped from mine and I could see a faint tinge of color come over her cheeks. She turned to Ives and said in a very definite voice, "No, that wasn't it at all. The one I heard had a higher voice."

29

"You're sure?" Ives asked her. "Just what was the difference?" He seemed a little disappointed from his words, but you couldn't tell from his manner.

She was still not looking at me. She was still looking at Ives as she answered him, but the color was still in her cheeks.

She said, "The voice I heard had just about an average pitch for a man. This one is unusually deep—it isn't one you would forget."

Ives grunted noncommittally. He got up and said, "That settles that." But he hadn't done with me yet. He turned to me and took the necklace out of his pocket and was about to continue questioning me when the door opened and a man came into the room. He was young, around thirty, blond and well built, and he just missed being too handsome. He still had his topcoat and hat on as he came in, and when he caught sight of her he threw his hat in a corner and crossed the room to her without a look at anyone else and then she was in his arms and he was stroking her head and saying, "Janet, baby, I came as soon as I could." It was then that I noticed the wedding ring on her hand.

Ives was looking at his watch and saying, "Ninety minutes from Santa Barbara is pretty fast going, Mr. Holbrook."

Janet raised her head from his shoulder—she was nearly crying again now and looked at Ives and said, "Begg, this is Lieutenant Ives and Sergeant Wilson from homicide."

He nodded to them and told Ives, "Montecito—it's a shade closer and that helps." He looked enquiringly at me and she said, "This is the gentleman who found—" Her voice broke a little and she couldn't go on.

I said, "My name's Foraker," in automatic fashion, maybe trying to help her out, but I don't think he heard, he had already started to comfort her again. He was saying to her, "I know, baby, I know . . . Maybe you'd like to go lie down a while—I'm sure these gentlemen wouldn't mind—" He turned to Ives, but she said in a surprisingly firm voice

30

before Ives could speak, "I'd rather stay, I don't think I could ever rest again till we've found who did that to Letty."

There was a little silence as though each man in the room were respectfully understanding her feelings, and then Ives slipped his little book from his pocket and took out his pencil and turned to Holbrook and said, "Your full name is—?"

He said, "Francis Begg Holbrook." He said it with a certain quiet dignity that I liked in spite of myself. Ives took it down and continued his questions.

I wondered why he kept me there as well as her, all of us in the room together, but I realized he still wanted to ask me something about the necklace, and he probably wanted her for all kinds of things which might crop up. And yet I had an idea, or rather not so much an idea as a feeling, that he liked to have us all together to watch how we were to each other. He seemed a great man for watching, and he had trained Wilson into that too, for Wilson was standing just where he had been all along, not saying a word, just watching.

Ives asked, "I understand you've been staying in Santa Barbara, or Montecito rather, for the past two days?"

"Yes."

"Where were you staying?"

"At Mr. Stephen Farnum's house."

Ives turned to Janet.

"That is the number you called him at just now when I told you the news?"

"Yes," she said.

He turned back to Holbrook.

"You will realize, Mr. Holbrook, that these questions are purely routine, that I have to ask them. . . . Now then, I take it that there would be somebody who would verify the fact that you were in Montecito at four o'clock this afternoon?"

Holbrook looked at him. But even Francis Begg Holbrook couldn't succeed in looking at Ives like that. Ives had something you couldn't touch, not even if you were the Emperor of China. Holbrook gave ground. He answered Ives straight, without protestation.

He said, "Yes, Mr. Farnum would. I was with him."

Ives nodded.

"Thank you, Mr. Holbrook." He turned to Wilson and nodded again and Wilson left the room.

I realized Wilson had gone to call Stephen Farnum, and I wondered why Ives was making such a play about the thing and it occurred to me that perhaps he was trying to make me feel safe and snug. I had a strong feeling that he had not finished with me yet, in spite of her saying it wasn't my voice. People can make the darnedest mistake about voices, especially wrought-up women. I didn't know if I was right or not in my train of thought but that was how it went just then.

Holbrook said, "But why four o'clock, Lieutenant? Do you mean it happened then?"

He got Ives's nod and turned to Janet. "But you didn't call me till just now. What happened?"

Janet said, "I was at the beach, Begg, I only got back after dinner and I called you directly Lieutenant Ives told me."

Ives turned to Holbrook.

"We have been given to understand," he said, "that your sister-in-law was in distress about some personal matter and that this is the reason why she became engaged. Can you give me any help on this—do you have any idea what was troubling her?"

Holbrook stood thinking. "The reason why she became engaged?" He turned to Janet in a puzzled way, with a look of inquiry that needed no words. She gave a little shrug and shook her head.

"I don't know," she said. "Letty never said anything to me."

Holbrook said, "If she didn't say anything to you she

32

wouldn't have told anyone else." He turned back to Ives. "It's the first we've heard of this, Lieutenant," he said. "Might I ask from whom you got this information?'

Ives said, "Yes, I can tell you that—it was from Mr. Marble, her motion picture director. He had found her work falling off and he drove her home on Monday night and she told him then. He said she was in considerable distress about the whole thing. You never got any hint of this, Mr. Holbrook?"

Holbrook shook his head. "Not a hint of it," he said. "She had been staying in the house too of late and you'd think one of us would have noticed—of course she wasn't quite her usual self for the past week, but naturally I put that down to the fact that she had fallen in love. And now you tell me she hadn't. I find that hard to credit. Even if it were true she'd hardly have told anyone else before telling my wife. They were very close—" He broke off a moment with a look at Janet but she was taking it steadily, she was taking it very steadily, so he went on, "Have you checked up on this Marble—I mean, after all, it seems very strange to me, knowing Letty as I did, that she would confide in anyone to that extent. Maybe it's just his story—you say he drove her home one night?"

I felt something hard inside of me. I was just going to say something when Janet said, "Begg dear, we can't expect to know everything about Letty's affairs. Perhaps there was something that she never mentioned to me. There may very well have been for that matter."

I wondered why she had said that. Somehow it seemed strange that she had said that. I was still thinking about it when Begg Holbrook went on talking. He said, "Well, I think it's very odd that Letty should have been so worried as all that and told a stranger. If you ask me, either she was worried and would have told us, or she wasn't and therefore his story is made up. What do you think of that, Lieutenant?"

Ives said evenly, "I think you can rely on the police to

33

check thoroughly on everyone, Mr. Holbrook. We've been at it for some years, you know."

Wilson came in at that moment. It was almost as well timed as though Ives had pressed a buzzer after the remark he had just made to Begg Holbrook. Wilson said, "Okay, chief, Farnum says he was there."

I gathered Wilson didn't like Begg Holbrook much more than I did or else he wouldn't have said that out loud.

Ives said, "Thank you, Wilson," and the look he gave Begg Holbrook had just the right nuance in it. "Thoroughly on everyone," it seemed to repeat.

Begg Holbrook said, "That's very efficient of you, Lieutenant. I presume you've also checked on Marble's alibi too?"

I said, "Mr. Marble happened to be directing a picture at the time."

He turned to me in surprise, but before he could say anything Ives's calm voice said, "As it happens, Major, Mr. Marble was not on the lot between the hours of three-thirty and four-thirty. He says he went shopping."

"And you mean you can't prove he did go shopping?"

"I do mean that."

I thought to myself that that was strange. I thought it was strange that a director would be away during a picture he was directing and I tried to remember what went on in motion picture studios from the little I had seen of them the times I went to have lunch with Tom. I remembered that once when we were having lunch they were all changing from one stage to another stage where they had different scenery set up for another scene and that process took a lot of time. It might well have been upon such an occasion that Tom took the opportunity to go shopping. I don't know why such thoughts should have gone through my mind just then, especially where Tom was concerned, but they did. They went through my mind all in a flash the way thoughts do, and then I saw that Begg Holbrook was looking at me again with some curiosity as he said, "You mean you know Marble?"

I said, "I do. I'm staying with him at the moment."

He was puzzled. He looked at Janet and asked her, "But I thought you said he was the man who found Letty?"

She nodded, and now she was looking puzzled too. They were both looking at me.

I said, "I know what you're thinking. It's a coincidence, it's a terrific coincidence, isn't it, that I should accidentally find someone who knew a friend of mine. I've been thinking the same thing. I quite agree with you, but there it is. Either you believe me or you don't, that I'd never seen her before."

Nobody said anything for a moment. Then Ives came back into the picture, not that he had been out of it exactly in the sense that I knew he had been watching me along with the others, but now he took up an active role again. He took the necklace out of his pocket and handed it to me and said, "Tell me, Major, you probably know more about these things than I do. Would there be any way of tracing the man who made this, from what you can see?"

I took the necklace from him and looked at it. I wondered what was in Ives's mind, why he had brought up the subject of the necklace just then. I knew Begg Holbrook was still looking at me and I knew she was looking at me too. I knew very well that she was looking at me as I looked at the necklace, and I didn't take my eyes off the necklace. I examined it carefully and I said, "The shells come from Guam. It is made with airplane wire. The man who made it is probably a good swimmer, especially under water, and a flyer—that is to say if it was the same man who dived for the shells and strung them together, and it probably was. Several of us used to make them in our squadron—"

And it was not until I had said all those words that my hands began to shake, ever so slightly, but they did begin to shake just a little, and I looked very carefully at the way

35

the wire was finished off in between the string of shells and the single pendant shell that hung from the middle of the total string, and I saw the thing then, I saw the one thing that I would never have believed, the way the wire was finished. There wasn't anybody else that I knew who finished them off in that way. I looked at Ives.

Ives was looking at me. His level stare was on my face, waiting, waiting. I wondered what to do. I looked at him carefully. There was something about Ives that I liked. In fact I had not yet come across anything about him that I didn't like. He made you feel that he was not a man to further his own career at the expense of justice. In other words he made you feel that he was a man. Ives had an integrity and it was written upon him if you knew how to read men right.

I looked straight at him and I said, "Ives, I don't understand this, and I can only hope you do. I made that necklace myself. I gave it away among the others I made, way back in nineteen forty-three."

His face didn't change and neither did his stare. He kept looking at me. After a moment he gave his characteristic little sound that was neither a grunt nor yet a cough but somehow a mixture of the two.

He said, "Who did you give this one to?"

"I can't tell. I made about a dozen. I can tell them by the way I twist the wire, but I can't remember each individual necklace, who got which one."

"You gave them to girls?"

"Mostly, yes."

Suddenly, she was standing in front of me. She was standing in front of me and her eyes were blazing.

"You did it," she said. "You killed her, you killed Letitia."

Nobody else moved, nobody else said anything. It was as though they were all waiting to see what I was going to do, how I was going to react. I was looking at her. I was looking at her and thinking, You poor kid, of course you have to

36

think that. And then I felt very sad, I felt very sad that she should be thinking that about me, and I looked back straight into her eyes, still feeling the sadness inside of me and I shook my head a little and I said, "You know I would never do a thing like that," and I spoke very quietly as though it were only the two of us together in the room. After a moment, as she returned my look, slowly the fire began to die out of her eyes and then I said, "You know it completely." And after a moment she said, "I don't know why I believe you, but for some reason I think I do, I think I do." And then she asked me with a puzzled look on her face, "But why did you pick her up if you'd never seen her before?"

I said quietly, "Would you rather I hadn't?"

She did not answer that. She did not answer it in words, but a certain look of understanding came into her eyes, or rather not of understanding but of gratitude.

But Begg Holbrook answered it, and there was no understanding or gratitude in his manner, none at all.

He said, "The hell you found her and picked her up. You never found her in Coldwater Canyon at all if you ask me. You and she had a quarrel about something and you hit her and killed her and then you brought her in to cover yourself up."

I knew Ives and Wilson were watching me. I knew I must not give away my intentions by any movement of the muscles of my face, and I moved my feet and body and hands so fast that I got to him and hit him before they could move. I hit him as hard as I could and he fell flat. He was out cold, there was no doubt of that. And then Ives and Wilson jumped me and had me by the arms and they started things, but I didn't try to resist them. I'd done what I set out to do and I didn't want to hurt anyone else.

Wilson said, "Shall I handcuff him?" to Ives and then Ives said, "I don't think that will be necessary, will it, Major?"

I shook my head.

"No," I said. "It won't be necessary, but you'd better see if I killed him or not."

She was already kneeling down beside him. She felt his pulse and opened his collar and then we were all kneeling down beside him. Even Wilson had let go of me when he saw that that was what Ives wanted. I was trying to figure out a whole number of things all at once and a kaleidoscope of thoughts was racing through my mind. I wondered about Ives, why he had behaved like that, and I figured that perhaps he was wise enough to deduce that my reactions were not the reactions of a guilty man. At the same time I was also trying to see how mad I had made her by hitting him, to see how badly he was hurt, and underneath it all to understand about that necklace. I decided to put the necklace out of my mind until I had found out about the other more immediate things. I couldn't tell from her face what her feelings were beyond the fact that she had obviously had too much to take in too short a space of time—in fact she seemed almost drained of all emotion just then as she knelt beside him.

There was some blood coming from his mouth, and as we were all bending over him I caught the smell of whisky about him. He began to stir a little and I could see after a moment that he was not badly hurt, just a couple of teeth and swollen jaw. Wilson felt him over and nodded and said he would be all right. She looked across at me, her eyes hard now, and said, "I hope someone will do that to you one day." She got up and got a water pitcher from the table and came back to him and dipped his handkerchief in the water and started gently bathing his face and dabbing away the blood.

Ives was watching Begg Holbrook as he came to. When Holbrook caught sight of me he started at once to get to his feet, but Ives put a hand on his shoulder.

"Take it easy, Mr. Holbrook," he said. "You're pretty shaken up. We'll take care of the Major all right."

38

"The sooner you get that murderer where he belongs the better. If you don't I will," Holbrook said.

Janet was still right by him, her arm round his shoulders.

"Try and rest, Begg dear, try and rest a little now," she said, and her voice was soothing.

Ives said, "We'll be going now, Mrs. Holbrook. Both of you try and get some sleep and I'll be back in the morning." He nodded to Wilson and me and we all went out.

She was still beside him the last I saw of her as we went out.

Chapter Five

I COULD NOT understand about the necklace. The thing was utterly incredible. I tried to think as Ives and Wilson took me back to the station. They drove silently, neither of them saying a word, and I had a little time to marshal my thoughts together before they started in on me at the station as I knew they were bound to do.

At first I could not think properly, with any clarity. My emotions were for a while so mixed up that they interfered with my thoughts. I did not know if it was she or if it was the necklace or if it was a combination of everything that had happened so swiftly, but as the car sped on down the avenue I found that I was literally unable to think as fast as I normally could when I was in a tight spot. I suppose there are a few times in everyone's life when this happens, when the synapse—the gap between thought and feeling—is sufficiently large to paralyze action, just as when a rabbit freezes in its tracks at the sudden proximity of an enemy. I think that the only reason I survived the war was solely the lucky fact that whenever this condition occurred in me it never precisely synchronized with the moment of the highest danger point, but came either just before it in anticipation of what I was about to go through, or just after it, so that in retrospect of the awful thing I had just been through, instead of being the victim of my enemy he became mine.

So it was now, thinking like this as the car traveled on, I became calmer and found that my thoughts were beginning to take coherent shape once again. One fact began to stand out in my mind most clearly, and that was that, while there could well be one coincidence involved, such as my coming across a dead girl who was a friend of a friend of mine, there simply could not be two coincidences as that same girl wearing one of my necklaces. Yet since both things were established facts, then one of them could not in all logic be a coincidence. There must therefore obviously be a logical explanation of the second fact, the fact that she was wearing a necklace which I myself had made.

I had reached this point in my thoughts when, at that precise moment, Ives asked me a question.

He said, "Did you ever give one of your necklaces to your friend Marble?"

I think we had reached exactly the same point in the same train of thought at exactly the same moment. I don't know how a thing like that comes about, but I have sometimes noticed it happening especially with two people who are in some degree sympathetic to each other, and I have thought that it is almost certain that there exists some form of thought waves, in the same way that radio waves or any other waves exist, and that this current is transmitted mutually to and from associated persons.

I knew instantly that I had to lie, and to lie well and truly. If ever a man has to lie, he should do it like anything else, 100 per cent.

I looked Ives straight in the face and I said, "No, Ives, I never did. I can see why you ask that. As a matter of fact I was thinking along the same lines myself, but it won't work because he never had one, I'm glad to say."

The whole thing, the whole of the awful thing, was going

through my head as I was speaking, and as I was saying the words to Ives my mind was racing, racing along a dark and bitter track, one that I couldn't bear to believe, yet one that I was forced to believe.

I remembered Elsa's words to me the first night I had arrived to stay with them, Elsa at dinner, she at one end of the table, Tom at the other, with myself in between them, Elsa leaning forward with that little moue of distress that she would wear if she thought she was going to hurt somebody, leaning forward and saying in a humble little voice, "Foraker dear, a dreadful thing has happened, I got your necklace out to wear when I heard you were coming and it's gone. I just cannot find it anywhere." And then Tom saying, "Yes, she even had me take up the rugs everywhere and look, but the darn thing has completely disappeared." And I saying, "Hell, Elsa, that's just one of those things. It'll turn up," and adding because I never did like people apologizing to me, especially Elsa, "Anyway it's Tom you should apologize to and not me, after all I gave it to Tom, you know. I didn't give it to you, now, did I?" And then we had all laughed because I had given it to Tom that night in San Diego when he and Elsa had become engaged so that he might give it to her and we all knew that perfectly well. We had kidded about it that evening on the terrace of the Coronado Hotel sitting over our martinis and looking at the sunset over the bay and I'd gone and got the necklace and given it to Tom and said, "This is for you, Tom, to give to the girl you love, and if you dare give it to anyone but Elsa I'll wring your neck."

I remembered that all in a flash as I was telling my lie to Ives, and I thought of something else too. I thought of something that had just happened that very evening, something that fitted all too well. Tom had told me that long story about Letitia's problem, some great problem which she'd had that had been the cause of her getting engaged. Yet her twin sister had known nothing about a problem, and you wouldn't think that twins as close as that would keep anything, especially anything that important, secret from each other. It fitted all too well. That the problem was the bunk—there was no problem except Tom's own problem when he found that the girl he was chasing had eventually decided against going through with it all. His being married would account for Janet and Begg's never having met him. It would account for many things . . .

Ives was saying, "In that case it leaves you behind the eight ball, doesn't it, Major?"

I said, "Yes. Yes, I guess it does."

We reached the station and parked and we all got out. They led me into the same room that they had taken me into before, only this time it was night, and they lit my part of the room with a bright white light. It was what I had been waiting for all along, the white lights. I had often heard about them and now this was it. I was determined to hold everything. I was determined they wouldn't get anything out of me about Tom. I had to see Tom first. I had to see him and face him with it and find out for sure that I wasn't mistaken. I was still for Tom, for some possible loophole. I could see no loophole now but I felt there must be one somewhere. I felt that neither Tom nor Letitia were that sort of people, and I knew darn well that if I couldn't see a loophole Ives certainly wouldn't, and Tom would be in it up to his neck before you could say Jack Robinson. I thought of Tom in a thing like that. I thought of Elsa and the baby, and thinking like that I found the white light wasn't going to be unbearable, nothing could be that unbearable.

Wilson started in. It was about the first time I had heard anything out of Wilson the whole evening, ever since he had driven me around to the house in fact. But now it seemed that he was on his own territory, a place where he had a certain amount of latitude from his chief, and he wasn't slow in taking it either.

He said, "Where were you this afternoon from the hours of one to four?"

I had not been expecting that question, but I gave the only answer that I could. I gave him the truth.

"I was at lunch with Mrs. Marble from one to about one forty-five or two o'clock. After that I wrote a couple of letters in my room at their house. After that— I suppose it must have been around three or so—I took the sedan and first I went to the post office and mailed the letters, then I went to a drugstore on Beverly and had a chocolate malt. That must have taken me till around three-fifteen. Then I went to the gas station near by and had the tank filled and after that I drove up through Coldwater Canyon Alley on my way to the hills. Must have been between three-thirty and four that I found her, I suppose. You know what time it was when I brought her in. Couldn't have been after four."

Wilson said, "I'm asking you to tell me what you did, not what I did."

I said nothing. I knew he was trying to get me wrong side up and I was not going for that. So I said nothing, just waited for him. He didn't care for that at all.

He said, "In other words you can't account for your movements from the time you left Mrs. Marble at two o'clock?"

"I've just done so."

"Who did you speak to in the drugstore?"

"The waitress."

"What did she look like?"

"A tired blonde who needed a permanent. Yellow hair and brown eyes."

"What did you say to her?"

"Chocolate malt, please."

"Anything else?"

"I already said she was a tired blonde who—"

"Cut that out. Who did you speak to in the gas station?"

"Man about thirty, dark hair, pleasant smile. I didn't notice the color of his eyes. I said, 'Will you fill her up and check everything please?' He said, 'You bet.' "

43

"Got a good memory, haven't you, Major?"

"I've never had any complaints."

"Then why didn't you remember your own necklace when you saw it round the stiff's neck?"

I counted one to ten. I counted one to ten inside myself calmly and evenly. Wilson had leaned forward a little on that last question and I could see his goddam face outlined in the fringe of the white light. I finished counting and then I said, "Because I had more important things to think about just then, such as looking to see if she was dead, looking to see how, looking to see any tracks, deciding whether to leave her there or bring her right in. But you wouldn't understand that, would you?"

Ives took over. He gave a little wave of his hand to Wilson and said to me, "Who did you give all your necklaces to?"

I don't know if Ives took over then in order to save time or to stop Wilson's getting mad before I did or to take advantage of my temporary upset, but I think it was probably a combination of all three factors. In his shoes I think I would have done the same, because it was good timing. I'd already noticed that about Ives. He was strong on timing.

I said, "I'd have to think. Do you want a complete list?"

"Yes."

I said, "Then give me five minutes without that light."

Wilson started to say something but Ives cut in fast.

"All right, Major," he said. He snapped off the big light, leaving a small low one burning in the corner of the room. "But don't forget," he went on, "I want that list complete."

I wondered if he already doubted my word about Tom or not. I realized he could very easily check up if he saw Elsa right quick, before I could get to her. But somehow I didn't think he did doubt my word. So far, as far as he was concerned, it had proved good to a man of his discernment, and I knew that. Besides he too had met Tom and must have judged him as an unlikely candidate for murder, although when you get right down to murder, and espe-

44

cially what the French call the *crime passionel*, then there are very few virile people who can be definitely ruled out, especially if they are matched against the provoking type of girl. But I couldn't think of Letitia like that, not the twin sister of Janet. Not unless the nature of each girl was quite different, one from the other.

I'd never come across such similar twins before, but I knew there were two types of twins, what they call one-egg twins and two-egg twins, the first deriving from the father and the second from the mother. I'd studied it in my embryology class and I'd met the second kind of twins several times and they could be just as different from each other both in sex and in nature as any pair of sisters or brother and sister born at different times. For the only difference between a two-egg twin and an ordinary brother and sister is that the twins happen to be born at the same time instead of one at a later date than the other. But the one-egg variety is quite another matter. There you really had something. They were literally one person cut in two, a splitting of the male cell into two parts. I didn't see how they could vary too much, one from the other, but of course I couldn't be sure. It was just a hunch I had. The only difference that I could see would be environmental rather than hereditary. But even if Letitia had been brought up by a bunch of thugs, while Janet had been carefullly sheltered in the bosom of a rich family, even so I couldn't believe that there would be too much difference in their basic personalities. That would depend upon how impressionable they were and they didn't strike me as being a very impressionable type. In fact she seemed to have plenty of character.

She. Here I was sitting in the police station in the welcome lull of the semidark and thinking of a pair of twins as she. Letitia and Janet. Janet and Letitia. I was getting all mixed up with myself. Maybe I needed some sleep. But first I had to think, I had to concentrate on necklaces, I had to think of all the people I'd given them to and it

45

was two years, easily two years, more like three years ago now.

I took out my handkerchief and wiped my forehead and got up from my chair and stretched my legs and got a pencil from the desk and took a sheet of paper from under Wilson's nose. I sat down again and felt better. I sent my mind back, back to a homecoming during the war. I was on the PBY coming into San Francisco, full with that quiet flush of a first leave, looking down at the Golden Gate, a bunch of necklaces in my hands that I was packing up before landing, and someone sitting beside me saying, "I wish you'd sell me one of those darn things, Foraker. I'm just a plain simple person and I need an edge like that with a girl." Sellick. George Sellick, that was his name. I gave him one because I had always liked George—he wasn't easy to get on with until you knew him well. One of those shy men who keep themselves to themselves as much as anyone can in a war, and I couldn't help thinking to myself as I gave it to him that even with a necklace he would find the going on the difficult side. I put his name down on my list for what it was worth. I hadn't seen him since then and except that he had been invalided out with malaria, I had no idea what had become of him.

I tried to think what other men I had given necklaces to, and I remembered the old man on Daytona Beach who had exchanged one for an Indian dagger—he said I reminded him of his son who was killed in the Pacific, how his son had said he was bringing home a necklace for his mother, and neither he nor the necklace had ever arrived and now here I was with a necklace, the same age as his boy, and so on, the way they do, the bereaved ones . . . I had given him a necklace and he had pressed the dagger on me, saying its bearer always bore a charmed life in combat and I was to have it in my plane. I did so later when I next went out. I wired it firmly in beside my instruments and I could always see it in the tail of my eye. . . .

I put the old man's name down, Admiral Gregg, and
46

tried to remember what other men there might have been, but there were no more, I knew that. The rest had been, except for Tom's and one for my mother, all given to girls. Girls that you met here, there and anywhere. I had often gotten quite a kick out of the fact that I would spend so long diving for the shells, then days and days in stringing them together, working away at them whenever we had spare time on our hands, and then giving all that away, just casually, to a pair of laughing eyes or a mocking smile or a moment in the moonlight.

I tried to remember all their names. Names and places, names and places . . . I eventually managed to get all the first names and a lot of the last names but for some of them I didn't even have their telephone numbers. I looked in my little book that I still had in my pocket, and got what numbers and addresses I could out of it. But they were not complete. The book brought it back, the heady times of the champagne days embossed in the middle of a war. Telephone numbers in pencil, in ink, one done in lipstick, scrawled in large girlish figures diagonally across the page. . . .

I counted them. I counted them all and found that they equalled the number of necklaces that I had made, eleven altogether, Tom, George, Admiral Gregg, my mother and seven girls. That made eleven. That was the complete list. That made ten for Ives, for of course I omitted Tom's name.

I got up and handed it to Ives.

"You won't find all the names complete and some have no addresses, but maybe you can trace them all."

I thought to myself, it was a fine thing to give the police the names of all your past girl friends, but maybe in a case of murder most of them would forgive me.

Ives said, "You don't quite seem to realize that it is important for you that we do trace them all, Major."

"Sure I do. But I can't help you any more than that."

Ives looked down the list. I was trying to make out just

what he thought was important and what he didn't think was important. Whether, in fact, he thought the list was important at all, or merely my reactions about the whole affair. He gave a little sigh as he scanned the list for the second time over, and then he beckoned to Wilson.

"Get this thing going right away. I want every necklace found." He looked at Wilson with an almost whimsical expression in his eyes. "After you've been able to trace all these ladies, of course. Use the Major as much as you need for that. He'll be on call at Mr. Marble's house any time you should need him for any identification purposes."

Wilson looked at Ives in his own bleak way. He started to say something, thought better of it, glanced at me and then went out.

Ives turned to me.

"I might tell you here and now, Major, that this is the most unorthodox procedure I've ever indulged in. But don't let that make you think it won't pay off in the end, whoever is at the bottom of this thing. Now you may go. And remain on call day and night until I clear you." And then he added softly, "Or don't."

I said good night to him and got up. I had nothing more to say to him or to anyone else that night. My mind was too full with Tom and Elsa, and above all I wanted to avoid them too and sleep a full ten hours before I tackled any other problems. I realized, as I hit the night air outside the station on my way down the steps to the car, that I was far, far more tired than I had been for many months, almost as tired, in fact, as those days and nights on Guadalcanal, so long, long ago. . . .

Chapter Six

WHEN I woke up the next morning it was already past eleven. I lay in bed for a good half-hour before getting up, thinking out my approach towards Tom and Elsa. I knew that by that hour Tom would be at the studio and that Elsa would be around alone and I thought to myself that in any case it was far better I should approach Elsa than Tom, although of course I did not for a moment intend to let her know in any way what it was that I was after. The whole thing was so delicate and Elsa so astute that for a time I wondered if I could ever make out on a matter of such delicacy, but I knew that I would have to try my best at it. I could not rest until I had proved to my satisfaction that it could not have been Tom. Yet if it had not been Tom I could not see how it could possibly have been anybody else, for the simple reason that the odds against any of my other ten necklace holders being connected with Letitia in any way were at least a hundred million to ten against, when you think that the population of this country is around a hundred and forty million. Statistically, therefore, it had to be Tom. Yet statistics is a curious subject, able to be more wrongly translated with greater facility than almost any other, just as logic when carried too far becomes a reductio ad absurdum, in true Germanic fashion.

I could see then, as I lay in bed, that if Ives thought that I had been telling him the truth regarding Tom's not having received one of my necklaces, then he would be up against this same statistical problem, unless, of course, he thought that I had kept one of them and given it to Letitia myself. The only other way in which his mind could be working was that I had told him a lie and that Tom or Elsa had received a necklace. In that case you would think that he would check up with them both before going much further. In fact, whether he believed me or not, you would think that his normal duty would consist in his doing this at the first opportunity. In fact, even as I lay there, he might already have contacted Tom at the studio or Elsa at home.

I got up and dressed. I realized that I should never have

lain asleep for so long, that I should have warned Tom before he left. Yet the problem was still of the same delicacy as before. For supposing he were guilty, he would still have to tell Ives that he had a necklace unless he were sure that I had previously denied it, and not only I myself but Elsa as well, and obviously he would know that she would not deny it. And if he were innocent, as I felt sure really must be the case although in some manner that I could not at the moment understand, then he would still say he had had a necklace because, knowing himself to be innocent, he would not lie about it.

There did seem to be one solution, presuming that he was innocent, and that was to risk telling the truth, and saying that he had to lie not only to back me up, for I myself might have stolen the necklace back, but also to protect himself and his family from the scandal which such an inquiry would inevitably bring to a man in his position. Elsa would certainly be on my side there.

As I left my room I found that I had thought so much about the whole thing and from so many different angles that now I had no clear plan in my head to follow at all and was completely confused about it all. I decided that the only thing to do was to leave things to happen as they went along with Elsa and trust to my instinct. I have often found that this process was the right one to follow, to think a thing out first and then to leave it to the unconcious to follow its own course in the subsequent action taken. Certainly it is a lot better than just to let life happen without thinking about it first, and equally it is often better than to stick to a rigid plan without regard to the invariably unexpected course that the turn of events provides in nearly every action in life, unexpected because in life one is dealing with another human being whereas in theory one is only dealing with oneself.

Elsa was in the nursery with the baby as I passed it on my way to breakfast. The baby was crawling at a good pace across the floor and Elsa was giggling at him. She looked up at me and I saw that for all her laughing with her baby, things were not as they should be with her. It was an impression that I got instantly, whether because of a quick gravening of her expression before she covered it up, or whether because of a slight air of tension that she communicated to me I was not sure, but I certainly felt that something had occurred to upset her.

We said good morning to each other, and she picked up the baby in her arms and came down with me to the dining room and sat at the table with the child on her lap while I ate.

I said, "This is the second meal running that we've done this—I'm not being the best of house guests."

"How did things go last night?" she asked me.

I told her everything that had happened at the Holbrooks' except for the necklace incident. I was also careful to skip any mention of my talk with Tom. She listened very carefully to all I had to say. When I came to the part about Begg Holbrook she paid particular attention and since I was unable to mention the necklace the picture made Holbrook's case look worse than it had.

She said, "It sounds like the husband to me."

"I've been thinking that too," I told her, because I had. "But would you tell me why he would kill his wife's twin sister, and even if he had wanted to, how he could possibly have done so when he was in Santa Barbara at the time she was killed in Beverly Hills?"

"I don't know why," Elsa said slowly, "but how do you know she was killed in Beverly Hills? She could have been dropped there later, couldn't she?"

"Not much later because she was still warm, and also it still doesn't help with Holbrook since he has an iron-tight alibi. He was a good ninety minutes away and he has proved it. Besides what possible motivation could he have for doing such thing?"

"What motivation did he have for picking a fight with you?"

I couldn't tell her about the necklace so I changed the subject. "What I don't understand," I said, "is why Tom was so upset last night."

She looked at me.

"I was going to ask you that," she said. "He sent me out of the room if you remember."

I said, "It seems he was afraid about me and I suppose he thought the two of us together in such a case would be better. The coincidence of my meeting someone he knew like that was a little startling, I guess. But chiefly I was unable to explain to him why I picked her up. I couldn't tell him what I told you, somehow."

She sat quiet a moment.

"I wondered," she said in a strange and overdeliberate voice, "if Tom had been seeing more of that girl than he had told me."

I watched the baby in his mother's lap trying his best to push a tablespoon down his throat. He had his mother's eyes and hair but he had his father's head, his head was shaped very much like Tom's head. I was thinking to myself what to say, what had provoked Elsa of all people to talk like that, and I sat very still for a moment not even continuing to eat.

I said, "What makes you say that, Elsa?"

She looked very frankly at me and said, "Things have not been the same between us since he came back. I suppose we're not the only couple but—that doesn't help exactly."

"How long has this been going on?"

She gave a little shrug.

"Oh—in a way I suppose it's been there ever since he came back, though we didn't either of us really know it for a while. I expected him to be the same Tom who went away and he expected me to have changed with him. Maybe it will turn out all right in the end but right now it's a bit trying to put it mildly. When it comes to sending me out of the room to talk about a girl it's going a little far. I don't

52

know if I can take that sort of thing much longer, Foraker. In fact, if it weren't for Peter—" she fondled the baby's hair, running it through her fingers and letting her voice die away.

I sat thinking. I'd had no idea. And now it looked worse than ever for Tom. I felt mean now, mean to be dragging things out of Elsa like this on false pretenses, but I could not possibly tell her anything about the necklace. I wondered how to handle the thing. I couldn't imagine Tom's having changed toward her in any way. In fact the idea of the war's having affected Tom in any way struck me as ludicrous, but on thinking it over I could see that that outlook was a purely superficial one on my part and that just because Tom was a more phlegmatic type than I didn't mean that he too could not be affected by war to some degree. In fact when you came to think of it, it would be amazing to find anyone at all who was completely unaffected by such a fundamental uprooting as war.

I switched my thoughts back to practicalities. I had to make sure somehow about that necklace. I knew that at any moment Ives might contact either Elsa or Tom about it. And, too, I could not sit any longer without saying something to her, making some kind of comment on what she had been talking about.

I said, "Tell me, Elsa dear, do you really think Tom has changed fundamentally since the San Diego days?"

"I suppose not," she said after a moment's thought. "I suppose if I really thought he had, I wouldn't still be sitting here. But I do think he saw more of that girl than he told me."

Here was I trying to pump her and get the conversation around to San Diego and the necklace and instead she was trying to pump me, trying to find out what Tom had said about Letitia.

I said, "He said something about her, that he had met her through her work and that because it was falling off he had had a talk with her, and naturally he was shocked at her

53

death but I think you're making too much of it, Elsa, I think you should think back to those San Diego days—remember the night you got engaged and I gave him the necklace for you?"

Her expression clouded over a little, and she moved her chair back and put Peter on her hip.

"I hardly think this is the moment to reminisce about that." She got up. "Besides," she went on with a swift gathering of herself back to her normal balance, "it's time for Peter to get some fresh air."

And that was that. I thought that the next thing I'd better do would be to go and see Janet and try and pump her about that problem. If Letitia had really had a problem then that made the picture look brighter for Tom. And, too, Janet might well know answers to a number of things which would help clear things up in my mind.

I was on my way out when the telephone rang. It was Tom. He wanted to speak to me, he said, and he was glad I had answered. He asked where Elsa was and I told him she had just taken Peter out for his walk. He said he would be right around and please for me to await his return. Then he said that if Ives called up in the meantime and asked me if I had ever given him or Elsa a necklace that I was to say no. And then he hung up.

I sat down and tried to figure it and failed. I got up again and walked around the downstairs rooms of the house and waited for Tom. When he came in it could not have been more than fifteen minutes, but it seemed an eternity.

He said, "Why didn't you tell me you gave Letitia Elsa's necklace?"

I looked at him.

"What makes you think I gave her Elsa's?"

"I knew Elsa lost it after you came. I knew you had no necklace of your own left. And Ives told me Letitia was wearing one of your necklaces and that you'd admitted it and that you had denied ever having given me one. Now,

54

Foraker, will you please tell me why you denied to me last night ever having met Letitia?"

I said, "Tom, you mean you denied to Ives that I'd given you a necklace in order to protect me, was that it?"

"Of course. I wanted to tackle you first. Why did you—"

I interrupted him.

I said, "Does it occur to you that I lied to Ives for the same reason you did—in order to protect you?"

There was a long silence.

Tom said slowly, "And you mean you thought I—?"

I nodded.

"And you never had met her then?"

"Never, Tom."

He sat down and tried to figure things out. I lit a cigarette and watched him and tried to think too. He was genuine enough, as far as you could tell with Tom. And I had always thought I could tell the whole way too, but since hearing Elsa's news about him my faith was a little shaken. After all, it could be an act, and it certainly suited Tom to deny having had a necklace if he were guilty, except that I couldn't see how he would know that Elsa would deny it too in case Ives questioned her.

Tom said, "This makes it different. I believe you for some cockeyed reason. I had been going to tell Elsa about the necklace to protect you in case Ives called her and asked her, but now that you don't need protection I'd just as soon not. You see, she might think I'd given Letitia the necklace myself."

I said, "Tom, it's none of my business how things are between you and Elsa, but there's this to consider. If you don't tell her about the necklace and then if Ives checks with her to see if I ever gave either of you one of them, she will say yes that I did. Now then, your goose will be properly cooked because you lied to Ives. Mine will be too, for that matter, but I don't mind that because I'm sure I can get out of it. Someone must have given her that necklace and in the end we'll find out who it was. But in the meantime you'll

55

be getting publicity which will ruin you in your work and you know it. I would advise you to tell Elsa so that she can deny it to Ives too that she ever had a necklace. It's stupid to go halfway in a lie, anyway. I know that may mean some kind of a private showdown between you and Elsa, but you'll have that coming sooner or later anyway if there's trouble between you, so you might just as well have it now and get it over with. And in the meantime we can find out who the dickens did give Letitia one of my necklaces if it wasn't you or I."

I didn't convince myself over my last remark—those statistics were still too much against it. I couldn't help believing that Tom had given her the necklace even as I was speaking, that in fact he had seen more of her than he had made out to me earlier. I wondered again about his absence during that afternoon when she was killed. It wasn't that I thought he had killed her, but I did think he knew more than he made out, whether this was partly due to what Elsa had said I don't know.

Elsa came in just then. She had Peter in his little gocart and she wheeled it into the front hall by the open door of the drawing room where Tom and I were talking. When she saw Tom she got a little more affable than usual in the way that she had when she was trying to cover up, and I could see that a situation had grown up between them since I had last seen them together.

She said to Tom, "Hullo, what brings you back so early?"

Tom said, "I just dropped in a moment to see Foraker. Something came up with the authorities, identification and so on, and I wanted to tell him what had been said."

"Is everything all right?" Elsa asked.

"Looks okay to me." Tom's voice had just the right ring to it as he walked over to Peter and started to make faces at him and poke him with his finger. Peter stared back at him with unblinking eyes and gave a chuckle that came from way down inside that tiny body of his. I caught a faint mist in Elsa's eyes as she watched them both.

56

The telephone rang just then. Elsa was nearest so she picked it up, and I was close enough to recognize that unmistakable quality that Ives's voice had, a little staccato and a little on the melodious side too. I couldn't hear his words of course but I waited for Elsa's reply and I watched her and Tom as I waited. Tom had stopped fooling with the baby and was standing very still. I knew he was waiting for the same thing that I was.

And then Elsa said, "Yes, this is she."

There was some more from Ives. It sounded like a question, but I could not be sure it was a question. I saw Elsa stiffen a little. There was just the slightest tensing of her body as she stood there with her back turned towards me, holding the telephone to her ear. And then her head turned a little and I knew she was looking towards Tom, although I could not see her eyes. I too looked at Tom now, and I saw that he was standing as still as ever, but now his eyes were on Elsa's and I could see that there was a passage between those two people, a passage of communication that could have been understanding or misunderstanding or a combination of the two. The whole thing took only the briefest instant of time. There was only the briefest interval of pauses in actual time between Ives's question and Elsa's answer.

She said into the telephone, still looking at Tom, "No, Lieutenant, I'm afraid I've never owned a necklace like that. Yes, I know Major Foraker made them but he never gave me one—I think he had given them all away by the time he met me, and anyway you know, Lieutenant, I was already engaged to my husband then. I hope there's nothing wrong?"

There was a little more from Ives and then she said goodby and hung up.

She was still looking at Tom and standing very straight now after she had put down the telephone and she said, "I guess there isn't much to say except I'll get it over with as soon as possible." And then her eyes fell on Peter and

57

she looked for a moment as if she were going to break right there, but she didn't. Instead she picked him up in her arms and then she said with her face half muffled against the baby clothes, "I do think you might have given her some other necklace."

Tom didn't say anything. He just stood where he was and didn't say anything, his face very ponderous now, in the way that it would go when he was in a spot. He always looked as though he were just about to read the minutes at a very respectable board meeting of company directors whenever he was in a bad place. It took me a long time to realize that about Tom, and when I first met him I couldn't get it at all, but once I got used to it I could tell just what that expression meant, and I knew now that that expression meant that Tom was going through all kinds of hell inside himself just then.

I said, "Elsa, how do you know that it wasn't I who gave Letitia your necklace?"

She looked at me a moment and now I saw that her eyes were moist and she gave a little half-smile through her tears and shook her head a little and said, "No, Foraker, not after what you told me about you finding her last night and how you felt. I know you too well to think you were doing any acting with me last night."

And then she left the room carrying Peter, and Tom and I were alone together as we had been before she came in, but now the atmosphere was quite different between us, for I too was now convinced that Tom had given Letitia that necklace, and I didn't like it, I didn't like it at all, however sorry I might be feeling for him. And so I too left the room.

Chapter Seven

IT WASN'T that I thought for a moment that Tom had killed Letitia, and I knew that Elsa did not think so either, but whoever had done so had in my opinion probably done so through jealousy of her affair with Tom.

I decided to go and see Janet Holbrook and try to find out from her or her husband what man or men Letitia had been seeing before she met Tom. The sooner we could find out just who the man was who caused her death, the sooner would Tom be out of something which I knew might at any moment blow up in our faces.

As far as Ives was concerned I had a perfect reason for my otherwise seemingly strange conduct in making inquiries of the Holbrooks. The fact that she had been wearing one of my necklaces was enough to satisfy him on that point. And it would look to Ives even better from my own personal security point of view that I should be making my own investigations than not, because if I were the killer I would be unlikely to do so.

I called the Holbrooks' house and got straight on to her. I recognized her voice directly she spoke. It was soft and cool and honest.

"Hullo," she said.

I said, "May I speak to Mr. or Mrs. Holbrook please?" Her voice got hard as she recognized mine.

"This is Mrs. Holbrook."

I said, "Good morning, Mrs. Holbrook, this is Major Foraker."

"Yes, Major Foraker?"

I thought to myself that I would have to be very good indeed to talk her into seeing me, judging by that tone.

I said, "I called to ask after your husband."

"My husband is in bed. He is not feeling very well, Major Foraker, as you may appreciate."

"I'm sorry. Is there anything I can do?"

"Not a thing, thank you."

"I'm truly sorry to have distressed you. I guess I was pretty strung up."

"Evidently."

"He did call me a murderer, you know."

59

"The whole thing is quite unimportant. I have other things to be concerned about just now as you should know. Good-by, Major."

"Wait a moment, please. It's about that that I wanted to talk to you. Perhaps you would let me come round for half an hour or so?"

There was a pause.

"You mean something about—about Letty?"

"Yes."

"Why can't you talk to the police?"

I thought a moment. I knew I couldn't tell her the truth about its being Tom's necklace and I knew I had to think of a reason to satisfy her question.

I said, "She was wearing a necklace I made. You must know that puts me in a very bad position with the police. Please let me see you. After all, I can probably help."

"Do you mean you can tell me something you daren't tell the police?"

I thought hard. I hadn't realized quite how smart she was, but I should have known how sharpened all her senses would be in such a situation.

I said, "I can't say anything over the telephone."

That did it. She said, "Come around in half an hour," and hung up.

On my way over to the house I thought of my approach. I knew it would have to be good. And I knew I did not have too much time before Wilson found the necklaces. Somehow I had a good deal of faith in Wilson's sleuthing abilities and I had a hunch that he would trace them all down within a matter of days, after which my position would be much more unpleasant.

There were no police cars outside the house. I wondered, as I rang the bell and waited, what Ives was doing. There were so many angles—he might be at the studio checking up there, he might be anywhere.

The maid opened the door and showed me into the same room where I had been the previous night. The

60

previous night. It seemed incredible, coming into that room again, that it had only been the previous night. It seemed aeons ago.

She was standing by the window. It was the first time that I had seen her by daylight. I had seen Letitia by daylight, but Letitia had been dead. I had imagined her alive in the sunlight but I had never seen such a thing, and until you actually see a thing like that you cannot realize even the half of what you will experience in sensation. I looked at Janet alive in the daylight and I knew that nothing I had imagined approached the real seeing of her.

I said, "It is very good of you to see me, Mrs. Holbrook. I think I know of something which may help."

She came a step towards me. There was a look in her eyes that made me feel a heel for having raised hope. You could see she had been thinking of her sister all through the night.

She said, "What is it?"

"Let's sit down," I said. "This may take a little time."

She looked at me, doubtfully. I sat down without waiting for her. I knew she would have started in about my talking to Ives again if I had not sat down quickly and kept the upper hand that way.

After a moment she sat down too and waited.

I said, "The thing is this. Someone who had received one of my necklaces was seeing your sister. This much we know. Now am I to understand that you would definitely recognize his voice if you heard it?"

"You mean you know who it might be and don't wish to tell Lieutenant Ives?"

I looked at her straight.

"I didn't say that at all, Mrs. Holbrook. I must ask you to go along with me a little way in this thing. Later on perhaps you will see why."

She sat thinking. She had a way of sitting with her head a little cocked on one side and I received a strange feeling in me as I looked at her. I felt that here is a girl, here is a

61

girl for me. I felt here is a girl who is strong enough to afford to need protection. She is thinking her problems out as clearly as she can on her own hook, but it is only a little hook and mine is bigger, and therefore it is logical that I should protect her as much as lies in me.

Sitting there so close to her, I found my swift thoughts becoming chaotic. I thought to myself, what is the matter with Foraker? I thought, it is Tom who needs protection, you had better be careful what you say or you will get Tom in a bad place. Why should you get all romantic about this woman? She is somebody else's woman anyway—she cannot be yours.

She said, "You know, Major Foraker, I trust you already much further than I should. I don't know why. It's a feeling, I guess. But I can't be expected to go too far in my feelings where Letty is concerned. Now I've been perfectly frank with you, and I shall expect you to be the same with me."

I said, "Thank you. Then I shall be frank. It isn't that I'm trying to conceal anything from the police. On the contrary, I have every reason to find the murderer as soon as possible. And I think that by talking with you who knew your sister where the police did not, I shall be able to piece things together with you much quicker than they can."

It was the best I could do in that particular line just then and I could only hope she would believe me and play ball. I knew for certain now that I could not possibly afford even to hint about Tom in any way. And I didn't feel too badly about what I had said really, because, apart from the Tom angle it was perfectly true—I did think that she and I together could dope things out faster than Ives, and with more chances of a quick success.

She said, "Well," and she looked at me carefully a moment and then she said, "we can try." I could see she had reached a temporary decision on that at any rate and so I seized on what advantage I had as fast as I could.

I said, "About the problem she had which Captain

62

Marble mentioned, both to me and to the police, haven't you any inkling at all as to what that might have been?"

She did not answer me and I got an instantaneous feeling that somehow I had put a foot wrong, but just where I could not tell. And then she said, "It does seem strange that she should have spoken of anything so personal to Captain Marble if he was only just her director, doesn't it?"

I said quickly, "Surely you're not implying that your sister—"

She cut right in, "I'm not implying anything about Letty, Major Foraker. I'm implying that Captain Marble could not have got such a thing out of her, if there were such a thing as a problem, mark you, unless he had wheedled it out somehow. Letty was never a talker about herself."

"Then isn't it conceivable that she spoke to nobody, not even you, about this thing which could have been very serious, so bad that eventually it broke her down to talk it over with a friend who happened to be along when the time was ripe?"

She thought hard about that for a moment and I added, "After all, she didn't tell Captain Marble *what* the problem was, but simply that she had a problem."

Janet sat thinking of Letitia, with a faraway look in her eyes. It was like a girl looking at herself in a mirror, yet at the same time with an affection and understanding that no girl could have about herself in a mirror. In fact the look contained both these elements, first of the girl thinking of another and then of the girl thinking of herself, so that it was the most complete look that you can see in anybody's eyes, that look that only a twin can have about a twin, a bond of duality not possessed by any ordinary mortal.

"Yes," she said at last, "yes, Letty could have done just that." She looked at me with a new interest. "Though how you could have known such a thing about us I don't know."

I did not answer. I simply looked back at her. And after

63

a moment she lowered her eyes and then swiftly changed the subject.

"You said something about my recognizing the man's voice. Did you have anyone special in mind?"

I said quickly, "No. No one special. But I wished to get clear in my mind whether or not you really could recognize the voice. For if you can, you see, it is going to help us a lot, since I know all the people who had my necklaces."

She must have accepted my words for she said, "But I thought you gave them all to girls, Major?" And her tone was not exactly sympathetic.

I said evenly, "Mostly to girls, yes. Not all."

"You mean you gave some of them to friends of yours, such as Captain Marble for instance?"

I didn't know why she said that—I suppose it was an obvious lucky shot. I said, "As a matter of fact I gave one to a George Sellick who was in our squadron, and I gave another to an admiral in Florida who had lost his son. I also gave one to my mother, but I don't think we need worry about that one. Of course it might have been a friend of one of the girls."

She ignored the last sentence. She said, "What did this George Sellick's voice sound like?"

"Normal pitch. Like many others. Hard to distinguish in words I'd say."

I was thinking to myself that Tom's voice could be described the same way. It could easily have been Tom's voice. For that matter I was darn sure it was Tom's voice.

She said, "Well, didn't you tell all this to Lieutenant Ives?"

"Certainly."

"Then what is it you want to tell me you can't tell him?"

"I want to find out from you what your sister's problem was."

She didn't like that at all. Not at all. She had that same hard expression as she looked at me that she had had the evening before when I hit her husband.

64

She got up and stood straight and said, "I'll trouble you to get out of here. You lied to me when you said you knew something you couldn't tell the police just to come in here and ask questions, questions about my sister."

I sat right where I was and looked at her.

"No more than you lied when you said last night you didn't know of any problem your sister might have had. I know you were lying now. At the time I wasn't sure but now I am. If you'd tell me we might be able to figure something out."

"I refuse to discuss my sister's personal life with you. I'll trouble you to get out."

"Then you do know, don't you?"

"Do I have to get someone to throw you out?"

"She was in love with someone, was that it?"

She sat down suddenly. She looked at me and said, "What are you trying to do?"

"I'm trying to find out who killed her."

"Then find who gave her the necklace, because he did it."

"What makes you so sure of that?"

"Because—" she checked herself and looked at me. "What do you mean? Are you trying to say that the man who gave her the necklace is not the man who killed her?"

"Yes."

She stood up suddenly again.

"You know who it was. You know who it was, don't you? And you're trying to protect him. It was a friend of yours. It was Captain Marble, that's who it was. And he murdered Letty when she refused to marry him—" she checked herself suddenly.

"Tom's married, and I know he would never have killed her."

Suddenly I saw what I had said. It was too late to get it back. I got up quickly and went across to her. She was standing like stone. I put a hand on her arm, or rather I started to put a hand on her arm but she was standing like stone and I let my hand drop to my side. I said, "Look,

65

you must believe me about Tom. I know he gave her the necklace, but I know 100 per cent that it just isn't in his character to do a horrible thing like that."

It was no good. I could see right then and there that it was absolutely no good at all.

I tried another way. Suddenly I thought I saw a way, from what she had just said.

I said, "What makes you so sure that the other man didn't kill her out of jealousy about her being with Tom?"

At first I thought that she hadn't heard me, she was standing so still and so intent upon her own thoughts about Tom that were inside of her. But she must have heard because after a while she answered me, and the words were clear and definite.

She said, "Because the other man wasn't in love with her."

I looked at her.

"You mean you knew all about this and you didn't tell the police?"

"It's none of their business. It's nobody's business."

"Doesn't it occur to you he might be the one who— killed her?"

"I've just told you he wasn't in love with her."

"You can't ever be sure of a thing like that."

"I'm quite sure."

I could tell she was sure by her voice, by her stillness and the whole way that she was standing there in front of me.

"How can you be so sure of a thing like that?"

She knew I had the upper hand. I knew she knew that I could easily tell Ives myself if she didn't satisfy me. I knew and she knew that she had to tell me how she was so sure, and she saw it then.

At last she said quite simply, "Because he is in love with me, that's how I am so sure, Major Foraker."

For a moment I couldn't quite take it in. I couldn't
66

quite take it in that Janet would have a lover, not Janet somehow. And then I saw that there was a loophole to that and I asked her, "Are you in love with him? I suppose you're not, because if you were you would not still be married to your husband. You would get free. You would, wouldn't you, Janet?"

It was strange just then. I don't believe either she or I noticed that I had called her Janet. I don't believe either one of us noticed it at all just then.

She said, "Yes, I would. I would not stay with someone I did not love."

I was thinking about all she had said. I could see the whole picture now, Letitia's problem, how she was in love with a man who was in love with Janet whom Janet did not love because she loved her husband. I saw how Janet could of course never have told Ives about that because it was none of Ives's business, how she could never even have told Begg about it because of loyalty to her twin sister and how that would account for her telling Begg she knew of no problem and how it would account for Begg's own ignorance of Letitia's problem too. But the one thing I couldn't see was where it left Tom.

I said, "Now I can understand why you think Tom killed her, presuming, as we both do, that it was he who gave her the necklace. You think he killed her out of rage at being refused in the end. You think that Tom twisted her story just a little bit, don't you, that the man she was considering marrying to avoid her unrequited love was Tom himself and not someone else and that when she finally decided against him he killed her in rage, is that it?"

She nodded.

"Certainly, how else could it have been?"

I said, "I don't know how else it could have been, but I'm darn sure Tom wouldn't have done that. For one thing, as I said just now, he's married himself."

"Is he happily married?"

"They've got a baby and they're both very dear people."

"You didn't answer me. In other words they're not happy."

"Even if there is some trouble that doesn't mean—"

She said. "What is the Marbles' number?" and walked over to the telephone on the little table by the divan in the corner of the room.

"What are you going to do?"

She stood by the telephone, and I could see that the strain was truly beginning to tell now. Her face was white with it all, and in the black dress that she wore there was no relief of color or line, for its cut was a severe one and the only trivial factor about her was a little lace handkerchief which was tucked into the bracelet at her left wrist and which fluttered a little as she reached out her arm for the telephone receiver.

"I'm going to call Captain Marble and see if I recognize his voice or not."

"But even if you did, even if it were he who was with Letitia, that doesn't mean that he—"

It was no use. It wasn't that she exactly cut me short, but I could see as the words were in mid-air that nothing I could say would stop her, that there was nothing to do but give her the number. She just stood there waiting for me to tell her with her hand on the receiver, and I gave it to her. She dialed the number and I stood waiting with her, and I could hear the little sounds that came from the street through the half-opened window, the sound of an automobile driving by and somebody's footsteps as they walked along the sidewalk and also I could hear the humming kind of sound that is sometimes made by the tires of a bicycle on asphalt. I could hear nothing at all through the telephone because she was standing with it too far away from me to hear it, almost halfway across the room, but after a period of waiting what might have been thirty seconds and could not have been thirty years, Janet spoke into the receiver to somebody and she said, "Can I speak to Captain Marble, please?" then there was another pause, quite a short one this time, and she said, "This is Mrs. Holbrook speaking. I would like to ask him something about my sister, Letitia Lane."

After a while I could hear a man's voice saying hullo through the receiver and then Janet said, "Hullo, is that Captain Marble?" and then I saw a little puzzled frown come over her face as she stood listening to the reply, and then she said, "I'm sure you will forgive my troubling you Captain Marble, but I am most anxious for some help and I think you could give it to me." Tom must have said something more to that. I could hear a voice vaguely, but without hearing any words, and I could see the intent concentration upon Janet's face as it was poised above the receiver and the little lines of puzzle were still there in between her eyebrows. She said, "Can you remember by any chance what night it was that you drove her home when she told you about her problem?"

This time, after the reply had been made, she seemed to become a little more definite in her attitude and then she said, "Well, thank you very much Captain Marble, and if I want to know anything further I will not hesitate to call you. Thank you very much. Good-by."

She put the receiver back on the hook and stood for a moment alone with her thoughts, and then she turned to me and looked at me and said, "Do you know, I could almost swear that that couldn't possibly have been the voice I heard. Of course the telephone— But I could almost be sure that that wasn't the voice."

I didn't know what to think. I simply found myself unable to think at all. The whole thing was so utterly unexpected. I had thought that she was bound to say that she had no doubt that it was Tom's voice she had heard saying good night to her sister, and now I found that she wasn't sure, that in fact it meant that it couldn't have been Tom's voice or else she would have been sure. I knew she would have been sure if it had been his voice.

"In that case," I said, "it could have been that while Tom gave her the necklace, there was some other guy whom she was talking about and whom you heard saying good night to her. In fact Tom could have been telling the truth all along. But then why would he have given her the necklace?"

I found I had started walking up and down and was half talking to myself. She was watching me and now there was a certain understanding in her eyes.

"Did he say that he had given it to her?" she asked me.

"No, he didn't actually say so, but the thing's vanished. His wife got it out ready to wear when she heard I was arriving to stay with them, because I gave it to them when they were engaged. Then it vanished."

"And you didn't tell Lieutenant Ives you had given him one of your necklaces?"

"Not after I found that he knew your sister, no. It looked much too bad for him, don't you see."

She said, "Yes, but why didn't he tell Lieutenant Ives himself, or his wife? That certainly seems strange."

"Because his wife was protecting him and he was protecting me."

Begg Holbrook's voice spoke from the doorway.

"It certainly will look bad for all of you when I tell him, won't it?"

She and I turned together to see him standing there in the doorway. How long he had been there I don't know. It couldn't have been very long or I would have seen him. But he had certainly been there long enough.

Chapter Eight

HE WAS wearing pajamas and a dressing gown and his hair was tousled. His face was not pretty after last night. His pajama coat was open at the neck and you could see he had a soft and nearly hairless skin, tanned to a golden brown. His breathing was above normal and in those china blue eyes of his there was that hint of disorientation that will give eyes the appearance of being magnified and set a little astray.

Suddenly I knew he had done it. I knew it inside of me. It was a strange feeling, one that I could not explain. I could not see how he had done it since he had not been there, and I could not see why he would have done it, but I simply knew in my bones that he had done it, and I did not speak. I was very very careful not to alter my expression in any way for I knew that it could be dangerous for her in some way if he knew that I knew he had done it. It all went through my head and my heart in perhaps a couple of seconds and then I was thinking to myself that he was behaving very foolishly to act in such a hostile manner; if I were the guilty one I would be careful to act in a rational manner; but then I thought to myself that for a man to have been capable of such a horrible thing as striking a girl a blow like that, whether he intended to kill her or not, he would have to be in an unbalanced and irrational state so that in real life, as opposed to fictional representation of it, that same state would persist afterwards during his endeavors to conceal his guilt.

My mind was working now as it did in combat. The camera of my mind was clicking at extra high speed, geared so fast that it was able to synchronize with the speed of life and therefore able to penetrate the minds óf those about me, so that it could not only think with my enemy but also see behind those thoughts of my enemy's and know why he was thinking as he did and what he was going to think before he thought it himself. It is a strange sensation and can only be preserved for a short time before fatigue sets in, and the length of time of the combat is therefore of paramount importance. I did not wish to disturb this precious camera in any way, to jolt it out of synchronization by even the slightest flicker and now I looked away from him for a moment and looked at Janet and I saw that she was looking at Begg Holbrook, her husband, with an expression that was on the surface one of protective love, but was, unknown to her, a mask concealing a feeling inside her of bafflement, of considerable bafflement about him and about her feelings towards him although she herself was unaware of this matter. Only I was aware of it at the moment, for I was vitally aware of the workings of those in the combat, and suddenly I realized that although Janet genuinely thought she was in love with Begg Holbrook, her husband, actually she was not in love with him at all.

She said, "Begg, darling, you should be sleeping. What disturbed you?"

He did not even answer her. He looked at her and asked, "What is he doing here?"

"Major Foraker came to try and help about Letty."

He turned to me, and I could see that he was not in the least afraid of me, of my hitting him again. His eyes were bleak and brittle, and he said, still speaking to her as he was looking at me, "He wouldn't have come if he had not had something to hide, and now we know what it is."

I was careful to stand still and retain my silence and let her speak. She said, "But darling, I've just called up Captain Marble and listened to his voice, and that wasn't the voice I heard, I'm almost sure it wasn't the voice."

He waved his hand.

"You can't say such a thing. You said you weren't completely sure yourself. Voices change. It must have been one of them, either Marble or our friend here."

I still said nothing.

She said, "Why must it have been one of them?" She turned to me. "What was that other man's name, Sellick? Couldn't it have been him?"

This was new to Holbrook.

"Who is Sellick?" he asked her.

I said, "He was the only other man who received one of my necklaces, but you're right in thinking it was more likely

72

to be one of us two, Marble or myself, since I haven't seen Sellick in over two years and he might be anywhere. However they'll find him eventually and his voice can be checked too, if he doesn't account for his necklace."

"You gave his name to the police?"

"Yes."

"But you didn't give Marble's and nor did he."

"No."

He looked at her.

"Of course it must have been Marble." He nodded in my direction. "And he's protecting his buddy. And you're listening to him protecting the man who killed Letty. Give me that telephone."

I said, "Last night you were so sure it was I who killed her."

He took the telephone from her as she handed it to him and said to me as he picked up the receiver, "I still haven't ruled you out, and I don't think the police have either." He got the operator on the wire and said, "Get me police headquarters in Beverly Hills."

My thoughts were going fast. I was thinking what action I should take and I was thinking what was in his mind, given that my hunch was right. Given that my hunch was right, then he would be thinking that here was an opportunity for a "fall guy," but there was more to it than that. What was it that made him so sure I would not suspect him, what caused his irrational behavior in being so openly antagonistic, in other words? There must be some very strong motivation behind him, there must be something so strong that it overcomes any fear that I would suspect him. Of course he had a cast-iron alibi, the word of Stephen Farnum, but even so he would not normally want me to start doubting it by behaving in any way suspiciously such as his present vengeful behavior now was. Why was he then able to act in such a vengeful manner? It must be because he felt extremely vengeful against the man that Letitia had been seeing, it must be that he was in love with Letitia, that

73

was what it must be, and the force of his jealousy which enabled him to kill her would be the same force which would drive him to get the man whom Letitia had been seeing.

And then I suddenly saw something else too. I suddenly saw that, if he were in love with Letitia, then certainly Janet did not know this. Janet had just told me that Letitia had been in love with a man whom she could not marry. Janet had just told me that this man was in love with her, Janet. Janet had just told me that this was the reason why she knew this man could not be in love with Letitia. Janet had been talking about Begg Holbrook, her own husband with whom she thought she was still in love, who she thought still loved her but who actually loved Letitia whom he had killed out of insane jealousy because Letitia, in trying to escape from her horrible dilemma of being in love with her sister's husband, had been planning to marry someone else, anyone, just to cut the Gordian knot.

Janet had implied to me that it had not been Begg, her own husband, whom Letitia loved, but another man, in order to protect Letitia's memory. I could see it all now. And I could see, too, that I would have to tread very delicately indeed in order to extricate Janet from the total situation. She believed that Letitia was in love with Begg, yes, but she could not believe that Begg was in love with Letitia. It would not occur to her that this would be possible since she would naturally presume her husband to be in love with herself. And also she would believe that any love which he might seem to display towards Letitia would be simply the normal fondness and affection of a man for his wife's sister.

My thoughts had all been racing, racing ahead of me, ahead of everything, as I stood waiting for Begg Holbrook's call to be put through. I knew that my thoughts and my conclusions were all based upon the one single instinct that Begg Holbrook had in some way, despite his cast-iron alibi with Stephen Farnum, killed Letitia. But my hunch about that was so great that I could not help basing all my conse-

74

quent thoughts upon that hunch. And a great deal seemed to me to fit, a great deal seemed to fit only too well. I could see the whole thing with a horrible clarity. And I knew that it was essential for me to try and preserve that clarity for as long as it would take me to disprove Begg Holbrook's alibi and to make Janet see the truth. And not only just to make Janet see the truth, but to do it in such a way that when she saw it she would be out of reach of Begg Holbrook. The thing seemed impossible of achievement, especially in the light of my own bad position with the police and of Tom's bad position, a position which Begg was even now making worse.

He was saying, "I want to talk with Lieutenant Ives. It's urgent."

I waited. I looked at Janet. She was standing by Begg, and she was watching me to see what I was going to do. I sat down and took out a cigarette and lit it. I had to act two different parts at once. I had to act one part for Begg Holbrook who knew I was not the killer, if my hunch was right. And I had to act another part for Janet who had no definite proof that I was not either the killer himself or sheltering the killer. She seemed reassured by my action and turned towards Begg again to listen to his conversation.

He said, "Ives—this is Begg Holbrook speaking. About those necklaces of Major Foraker's. It seems he gave one to Captain Marble. Yes, I just overheard him telling my wife. He said he couldn't tell you because it would look bad for Marble if he did . . . Yes, he's here in the room now . . . Just a moment . . ."

He carried the telephone over to where I was sitting and handed me the instrument with a gleam of satisfaction in his eyes.

I took the receiver and said hullo to Ives. Ives's voice was not at all pleasant.

He said, "This puts you in wrong with me, Foraker. You get right back to where you belong and wait there for me. If Marble's there say nothing. And I mean say nothing."

75

The receiver clicked suddenly with the slam from the other end. He certainly meant what he said. I got up.

"He told me to get back, so I'll go now." I looked at them both, I was thinking hard how to do it right for both of them.

Janet helped me without meaning to. She was standing with a puzzled expression back on her face again now, the same expression that she had had earlier, and she said, "Begg, I still don't think I made a mistake over either of their voices. I still think it was somebody else."

Begg said, his eyes on me, "Somebody else who had one of his necklaces who also knew her? How could it have been? You made a mistake, that's all, honey. It was either Marble or our friend here who was going to marry Letty."

He had said, "was going to marry." He hadn't said, "who killed her." I don't think Janet noticed it. But I noticed it. And I knew that he was out to hang the man who had been going to marry his Letitia. And I knew I should waste no time in getting back and warning Tom of his danger.

I turned on my heel and left the room.

Chapter Nine

WHEN I got back, I found Tom still at home. He was in the study. And the whole place was upside down. Books had been removed from the shelves and strewn haphazardly about the chairs and floor, the furniture was pulled about, and he was in his shirt sleeves kneeling down behind the sofa in the corner of the room hunting for something on the floor.

He looked up as I came in and I could see at once in his face that he had been having great trouble with himself.

I said, "What is it, Tom, what are you doing?"

Even when Tom was in the greatest distress he still had his way of speaking in a steady tone, the delivery of his words was always calm, although the words themselves might not be.

He said, "I've hunted all over the whole of this goddam house for that necklace and I'm going to find it. Nothing else will convince her, and she says she is sure you didn't take it."

I said, "Tom, I made a bad mistake about you." I thought a moment, I thought of Ives on his way, of Elsa upstairs with the baby, Elsa crying with her child, hers and Tom's. I said, "Have you looked all over the house?"

He nodded, actually he shook his head from side to side slowly in the way he would sometimes do, and I knew it was a nod, a nod of despondence.

He said, "I've combed the whole place except the nursery because she's there, but I know she's looked there before, the day she lost it. In fact we both did."

I could see in his face that he was beginning to crack a little at the memory of that, at the thought of his trouble with Elsa, and I tried to think fast of something concrete to stop it, to stop in its tracks an oncoming wave of despair.

I said, "Say, Tom, if Elsa could see the necklace that Ives has she'd know if it was hers or not, wouldn't she?"

That did it. For a moment he looked at me, blankly, and then he began to brighten up. "That's right, Foraker, of course she would. But—but how can we do that? We've all said we didn't have one. We couldn't ask Ives to see it or he'd get suspicious."

I wondered what to do, how to put it, remembering that Ives had told me to say nothing of his coming.

I said, "I'll call up Ives right now and say that we have just remembered that one of my necklaces was given Elsa by a friend of mine before she met you and she didn't know it was one of mine." I was just talking fast to think out what to say, saying the first things that came into my head. I was still trying to think how to solve the thing with Tom when the doorbell went. Tom answered it. Ives and Wilson came in. They were looking tough.

Ives said, "Okay, now where's your necklace you denied having?"

He was looking at Tom, and Tom looked at me instantly in a bewildered and accusing way.

I said, "It was my fault, Tom—I thought you'd given it to her, just like Elsa did."

"You mean you told them that?"

"It came out when I was talking to Janet Holbrook and her husband overheard me and told these people."

Ives said, "Where is it?"

Tom lifted his hands, pointed around the room to show the shambles it was in.

"We've looked the house over, combed it."

Ives followed his arm round the room, looked back at him. He looked at me. He said, "I told you to say nothing."

"I didn't," I said. "This was happening before I got here."

"Why did you both deny having had one?"

Tom answered, "Because we each thought the other had given it to her."

Ives said nothing. Wilson said nothing. They both stood there, saying nothing better than most people can say it.

Tom said, "Why don't you show the necklace you've got to my wife? She would know if it was hers or not."

Wilson gave a short laugh, one short sound like the hollow rasping sound an old tin can might make if you threw it down the bottom of an empty well. You could still hear it after it had stopped, echoing around the walls of the room in the silence that followed, only maybe it was really only echoing around the walls of my heart, maybe you couldn't really hear it any more but in the imagination. He said, "He expects us to believe what she says. Now ain't that a dandy one?"

Ives paid no attention to Wilson. He was concentrating, he was concentrating on the situation before him, the immediate situation, to the exclusion of anything else, in the way that he did, watching Tom's face very closely, taking in

78

the shambles of the room, and I knew he had not missed a word or a gesture made by either of us since he came into the room.

He said to Tom, "Your wife believes you gave Miss Lane her necklace, doesn't she?"

Tom nodded.

"Yes."

"And it has caused trouble between you?"

This time Tom just nodded, a brief nod wthout any words, and there was nothing left unsaid in that nod.

"And she denied to me having a necklace because she thought you had given it to Miss Lane and wished to protect you?"

"Yes. But she didn't think I killed Miss Lane."

Ives said, "Did you give your necklace to Miss Lane?"

"No."

He said no more than the curt "no," just waited, his poise now quite recovered, or rather the mask of it. Inside I knew just what he must be feeling. Whatever readjustment troubles he might have had with Elsa since he came back from the war you could see that he had now potentially gotten over them, or would have gotten over them if it were not for the fact that now it was too late, that now the split with her had actually occurred. The day had been, I felt certain, such a psychological shock to him that it had rocked him back to his old even keel where he had been before the war, even during the war for that matter—that is, he was ready to be back on even keel if things went right with Elsa. But at the moment things certainly did not seem to be going at all right. In fact they were in just about as bad a shape as they could have been.

Wilson said, "Looks to me, chief, like we'd better take them both along to the station and find out some more." Wilson was always longing for his own ground, the ground of the bright lights in the little room in the station.

Ives started to say something, when the door opened, and there was Elsa. She showed surprise to see so many

79

people in the room. Clearly she had come down to speak to Tom and had expected to find him alone.

Tom said, "Come in, Elsa. Let me introduce Lieutenant Ives and Sergeant Wilson. We're all having a little get together here about your necklace."

She looked around at us all, then back to Tom. She went up to him, said in a quick little voice, "Tom, you must come, you must come up to the nursery at once." She looked around at Ives and said, "And I think you'd better come too, Lieutenant, I think you'll find this important."

Ives was frankly puzzled—we were all puzzled for that matter. But Elsa didn't wait. She turned and led the way out of the room and there was something in the way that she did it, an air of authority, or rather of certainty that we would all follow, which made us do so. It was strange, it was a very strange thing, the way all four of us just followed Elsa up the stairs without anyone's saying a word, not even Wilson. Tom went first, and Ives was behind Tom and Wilson was behind me, and as we went up I could hear Wilson muttering something to himself half under his breath, but I couldn't hear what he said, and anyway I wasn't paying much attention because my mind was focused upon what Elsa wanted us to see. She held up her hand as we got to the open door of the nursery and put her finger to her lips and Ives actually went on tiptoe to the door, in fact we all went on tiptoe to the door and looked in. I looked over Tom's and Ives's shoulders as they stood in the doorway next to Elsa, and Wilson stood beside me craning his neck to see.

Peter Marble had climbed up on a stool and he was playing with a brooch of Elsa's that he had evidently just taken from the dressing table which she had in the nursery. He did not see any of us as we watched him and after playing with the brooch for a while and holding it up in his hands and cooing a little over it he started to climb down with the brooch firmly clasped in his right hand. Somehow, more by luck than anything else it seemed to me, he made it down to the floor. Then he started across the room with it. You could see he had a purpose. I think all of us could see that he had a purpose in his little mind. He crossed the floor to the unit heating ventilator in the wall, and then he solemnly started stuffing the brooch through one of the holes in the ventilator. Everyone waited while he tried to get the brooch through the hole. After a while he made it, gave it a final determined push and then listened intently. There was a clang as the brooch went down the heating shaft, and a broad smile came over Peter Marble's face and he clapped his chubby hands together and gave a coo of delight. Then he turned and started back for the stool by the dressing table.

Elsa went after him and picked him up in her arms and turned back to Tom and came up to him and put her hand on his arm. There were tears in her eyes, but she was smiling. She said, "He's done it before, of course."

Tom didn't say anything. He just put his hand on hers, and then after a moment he looked at Peter Marble who was puckering, ready to cry at the unexpected interruption of his game. Tom poked him in the belly and then he said in the gruff tone he always put on to his son, "Cute little kleptomaniac, you."

Elsa turned to Ives.

"That's where I last put the necklace, on that dressing table. That must have been the first time he did it. Now today he's done it twice again. You saw the last time yourself."

Ives just nodded. He turned to Wilson.

"Have that shaft checked and see if the necklace is there or not."

Wilson didn't like that at all. But there wasn't anything he could do about it. It was obvious enough that it must be there, obvious enough even to Wilson. He was starting off down the stairs to the servants' quarters when I stopped him.

"Wait," I said. "That's one of those ventilators with a

81

handle. There's a ratchet inside, and there's just a chance you won't need to check the shaft. Give me a flashlight, Tom."

Ives didn't say anything. Nobody said anything. They just waited while Tom got the flashlight and I examined the ventilator. You couldn't see inside because it was dark and on the same side of the room as the window so that the light did not stream into it, but when Tom brought me the flashlight I flashed it inside the open ventilator and it showed the ratchet stretched across the middle of the opening of the shaft and it showed something else too, it showed a cowrie shell necklace caught on the ratchet and dangling down the mouth of the shaft. You could see it quite plainly in the light from the flashlight, Tom and Elsa could see it, and Ives and Wilson could see it too.

Wilson looked at Ives.

"How do we know he didn't just plant it there?"

I said, "And trained the baby, too, Wilson?"

Wilson turned on his most hostile look. He took a little book from his pocket and opened it as he looked at me.

"Okay, Major, this may let your friend here out but it doesn't let you out yet. No, sir." He checked down a list in his book and said, "This guy Sellick, George Sellick, we're having trouble tracing him. Where did you last see him?"

"I told you," I said, "I haven't seen him since he left the marines over two years ago. Is his the only necklace you've left untraced?"

Tom was staring at Wilson and me.

"George Sellick," he said. He turned to me. "But you didn't give that fellow one of your necklaces, did you, Foraker, George Sellick?"

"Matter of fact I did—he asked for one and I felt sorry for him. Why?"

I could see there was something in Tom's face, he was looking utterly taken aback.

"George Sellick!" he said. "*That's* who she was seeing then." He was speaking more to himself than to us. He

82

came out of it and said to me, "George Sellick came to see me at the studio just over two weeks ago, or somewhere 'round then. He brought the manuscript of a novel he'd just finished. I saw him in my office. I never cared for him much so I just said I would read it and got rid of him by asking my assistant to show him around the studio and take him down onto the set. He must have met Letitia there. And I've never seen him since. What's more, I've tried to see him, because we all like the novel and want to buy it. I made an appointment to lunch with him at the Beverly Wilshire where he was staying and he didn't show up. And that was the day she was killed. I know that because that was what put all thoughts of work out of my mind so that I've never thought to follow up on him since. Naturally I never connected the two because I had no idea that of all people you would have given him one of your precious necklaces. In fact I didn't even think to mention to you I'd seen him."

Ives said to Wilson, "Get the Beverly Wilshire on the phone and check up."

Wilson didn't need to be told. He was already making for the upstairs extension which stood on an occasional table in the passage, just outside the door.

Ives said, "What kind of man is this Sellick?"

Chapter Ten

I WAITED for Tom to answer Ives's question, because he had seen George Sellick recently and I had not. I remembered him as a man who was moody and kept aloof for much of the time. It had never occurred to me to think of him as a writer, but directly Tom had said that he was one the thing seemed to click. It made complete sense somehow, thinking of George Sellick as a writer, and even as a good writer at that. And it also made sense, and a great deal of sense, thinking of George Sellick as a possible killer. You could think of him as a killer who would kill in a sudden mood of maladjustment whereby the killing would be the only method of adjustment or relief from maladjustment presented at the moment of greatest tension. And all of us had been killing for a while anyway. Yet you wouldn't somehow think of George as being the man who had actually killed Letitia, not Letitia. Not unless I had Letitia all wrong. Of course Letitia had gotten herself killed, there was no doubt of that. And people didn't normally get themselves killed unless they were the victim type, that is, the sort of person who was apt to get killed by his own foolishness or through some fault or other which would render him more liable to be placed in such a position. I hadn't thought of her like that before. . . .

I could not quite understand the turn my thoughts had taken as I listened to Tom telling Ives about Sellick and Elsa quieting the baby who had started to cry and Wilson outside on the telephone talking to the desk at the Beverly Wilshire. Everything was happening all at once and I was trying to co-ordinate three different things occurring around me plus my own thoughts into one coherent pic-ture. I had a sense of strange urgency about it, as though somehow there was being presented to me in the course of those few moments up in the nursery a key which would give me the total picture. I had a feeling that there was something important and vital latent behind all the mani-festations of life going on around me at the moment, espe-cially when combined with the subconscious thoughts going through my own head. I knew there was always a rea-son for everything that happens in a person's mind, and I wondered desperately why my mind should be behaving just as it was at the time that it was. I tried to stand outside my mind and observe the four processes that were happen-ing, Elsa's face watching Tom, a little puzzled she was as she listened to Tom, as he spoke of Sellick and his movements, Wilson at the telephone finding out that George Sellick had left on the day of the death without checking out, and my own thoughts still in process about Letitia and the sort of person that she might have been. . . .

The idea of Letitia and George Sellick linked together was a strange and new one to me. It changed my concept of Letitia from what it had been earlier. Perhaps my concept of Letitia had already changed a bit since my meeting with Janet, her living sister, but now the idea of Letitia with George Sellick—that did change Letitia in my mind a little more. George Sellick was certainly not to be classified as a run-of-the-mill male. And for Letitia to associate herself with someone as strange as Sellick was surely a comment upon her own state of unbalance. Janet ascribed that to her being in love with her husband (she hadn't said her husband but that was who she meant), but I could not help thinking now for the first time a little uncharitably about the reasons why Letitia should have been in love with her sister's husband. Somehow I couldn't believe that Janet would have fallen in love with Letitia's husband. She wouldn't have let herself.

And now, on top of my thoughts about Letitia's character, I heard Tom saying something to Ives which was making Elsa look closely at him again, and it made me do the same thing too, for he distinctly implied that he and Letitia had seen each other again after their scene in the car on the avenue when he had advised her against marrying the man who now turned out to be George Sellick. And before he had always maintained he had never seen her again. Because now he said that she had told him that she had taken his advice and was not going to go through with the marriage and was going to tell her friend that at the earliest opportunity.

"When did she tell you that?" Ives sanpped at Tom instantly.

Tom said slowly, "She told me that when I saw her the day before she was killed."

85

"Why didn't you tell me that before when I was questioning you?"

Tom looked across at Elsa. She was standing waiting. He turned back to Ives and said, "Because I didn't wish it to become known, naturally. However, since it now has to I might as well come out with the whole thing."

"You certainly might as well," Ives said.

Tom started to talk again, and I knew he was talking to Elsa as much as he was to Ives. It was a strange situation. In a way it made me feel I shouldn't have been there. Certainly I was very glad for Tom's and Elsa's sake that Wilson was still outside telephoning. For a moment I wondered whether I should go out and join him, but then I thought that I would stay where I was because Tom had also lied to me about not having seen her again, Letitia. He had not said outright that he had not seen her again but he had very definitely implied that he had not seen her and that was the same thing. The only conclusion I could come to from his having done that in private with me was that he feared that even I might tell Elsa, and that hurt a little. Surely Tom could not think that I could ever do anything against him to Elsa, not unless perhaps he should have been thinking that Elsa's affection for me was more than it should have been. I had never thought of such a matter before but now that it crossed my mind for the first time it did occur to me that it was conceivable, in the state of mind that Tom had recently been in and with the trouble between him and Elsa, that it was conceivable he might have become a bit jealous of me with Elsa, and yet as soon as I thought it I determined to kick such a thought right out of my mind. It just wasn't Tom to be like that.

The only other thing I could think of was that Tom had not told me because he might have thought that even I would suspect him of killing her if I had known that he was overly mixed up with her emotionally. I preferred to think it was this that had stopped him from telling me rather than the other, and as I listened to him talking now to Ives I began to think that I was probably right, because it gradually came out in what he was saying that he had been more involved with Letitia than he had formerly admitted. It seemed that he had heard from her by telephone that day— at first it was not at all clear whether she had called him or he had called her. Ives asked him. He had to make it clear then.

It was she who had called him, and she had asked to see him concerning the matter they had been discussing. Tom had agreed to meet her—he made no excuses for himself over this as he was talking and I liked him for that and I think that Elsa did too, as least that was the impression that I got as she was standing there listening to him while holding the baby in her arms, waiting for him to finish. He said that then it was mutually arranged between them that they meet somewhere quiet and he had agreed to see her in a small restaurant on Wilshire where they would be unlikely to see anybody that they knew. Not, he said, that he had attached too much importance to this although at the same time he was not averse to the idea of reasonable privacy, away from the eyes of columnists. He could not have seen her at the studio since people knew she had left the picture.

When he met her he could see at once that she was still looking wrought up, although not in such a bad state as she had been before. They had had lunch together and she had told him then that she had decided to take his advice and refuse to go through with her prospective marriage when next she met her date. Then she had asked him what did he think she should do about her life to take the place of this marriage. He had asked her once again what was the problem which was so upsetting to her but she had still refused to tell him, saying that as yet she did not feel that she knew him well enough. She said she felt that she would have to concentrate harder now upon her work and asked him if he thought he might be able to do what he could for her in this respect in spite of the way she had previously let him down over it. He had said that he would do what he could. He said that he was glad that she had come to such a sensible conclusion. She said that although she realized it was what the world would call sensible, yet it was also a very painful personal position that she was in and she said that therefore she would need every possible buttress in the way of personal friendship that she could get in order to keep herself straight on the right mental track. He had said to that that he would be very glad to be a friend of hers. He had asked her again then to tell him her problem but she had again repeated that she could not tell him yet, but that perhaps later on when they knew each other better she might be able to talk more about the matter. It was at that point that he had suggested, and he admitted that he suggestion had come from him, that they should meet again at some future time after she had told her man that she would not marry him. A date was thereupon arranged between them for the following week. That, Tom said, was all that had transpired between them. The following day he heard that she had been killed. . . .

I caught a glimpse of Elsa's face just then before Ives started to question Tom further, and I could not quite fathom what her feelings were. I got the impression that she did not quite know herself, that she was still awaiting some sort of clarification, perhaps in order to make up her mind. Certainly she was not at ease about it, that was quite sure. And I, too, was not at ease about Tom either, when Ives started to put the questions to him which I myself was wanting to put also.

Ives said, "This is all very interesting, Captain Marble. Tell me, before we go any further, was Miss Lane aware that you were a married man?"

"I don't know," Tom said. "The question didn't come up."

"You didn't bring it in anywhere?"

"No—after all I have been her director for some time and I presume she would know I was married in the same way that anyone else on the lot would probably know if they've been there some time."

"I see. Then you presumed that she knew?"

"I suppose I did, if you put it that way." Tom went on. "And it's just because I knew you would put it that way that I didn't tell you this before."

Ives said, "Withholding evidence in a murder case is pretty serious, Captain Marble. The fact you did so suggests I am right in putting it that way."

I thought to myself that Ives was an extraordinary man to hit that particular nail on the head instead of going right on to show, as most policemen would have done, that it had even more serious implications.

Tom shrugged his shoulders.

He said, "All right, perhaps you were." And then he looked straight across at Elsa. From where I was standing I could see how straight he looked at her and I could also see how straight she looked back at him. And it was kind of nice. Seeing my two friends looking at each other like that gave me a good feeling because I could see, knowing them so well, that they were looking at each other with a great deal of understanding, the understanding that is in some marriages. And then Elsa put out her tongue at him, very quickly so that Ives shouldn't see, and Tom gave a quick smile and turned back to Ives, who was already started on his next question.

"And you mean to tell me, Captain Marble, that you did not see Miss Lane again?"

"How could I have done so? That evening I was home for dinner and she was killed the following afternoon."

Ives was really getting tough now.

He said, "And where were you then? You were not on the lot. You said you went shopping. Just at that time."

"I know I did. As a matter of fact I went to the Beverly Wilshire to try and find George Sellick. He had cut his lunch appointment at the studio with me. We were, and still are, most anxious to buy the picture rights to his book

89

before anyone else gets wind of it. That is why I kept quiet about it and said I went shopping. At that time I saw no possible connection between Sellick and Miss Lane as I have already explained. It so happened that at the time you mention I was in the Beverly Wilshire where I had gone personally to try to find out what had become of him."

Wilson had just come back into the room and he said, "That's right, chief. I just got all the dope and Marble was there as he says."

Ives turned to Wilson.

"What did you find out about Sellick?"

Wilson had a notebook in his hand. He started to read it.

"He left the hotel without checking out. Thursday, the day she was killed. Last seen early Thursday morning by a bellboy, Sam Keeler, who says he saw him buy a paper at the stand. He was wearing, as far as the boy can remember, gray flannel pants and brown sports jacket. Hotel wrote to the address he gave and so far has received no reply. That was today, Friday. Address given was Hotel Pierre, New York. No time for reply before early in the week after which, if unfavorable, they would have checked with us, usual routine. Description as follows. Six feet tall, black hair, gray eyes, hundred fifty pounds, distinguishing marks none. He left all his luggage at the hotel. There was no means of telling from it where he might have gone. Packing had not been done, clothes were left around, bed had been slept in as usual. All papers left at the desk, sealed, including typescript of a book. Papers were opened on my instructions and are as follows:

"Two movie stubs for the Fox Wilshire—I've checked the numbers and they say at the theater they were issued on Monday twelfth, four days ago. One Biltmore Theater program, *The Hasty Heart*, and one receipt from the Tovarich Shoe Store for nine dollars fifty-seven cents—I've checked on that and they have a record of selling a pair men's brown leather shoes, size ten, corresponding to that price, but the salesman who sold him is on his vacation up in Oregon for two weeks and no one there remembers the customer. Then there's a stub for the tennis matches at the Los Angeles Tennis Club dated Sunday eleventh, just the one stub. I've checked there but they can't remember who bought the ticket, it's one out of hundreds in the public stands. Those and the manuscript of the book are all the papers found."

Ives said, "Have you instituted the check on exits?"

"All taken care of. Air, rail and highway."

Ives nodded. He was thinking, and thinking fast.

He said, "We'd better make sure he did meet her. Have you checked with the Holbrooks on the name, any possible clue?"

"No, sir."

"Have them come round here at once. Both of them. I want to talk to them."

"Yes, sir."

Wilson left the room, and Ives turned to Tom.

"And you check with your assistant at the studio and see if he introduced them or not—Sellick and Lane."

Tom nodded, and Elsa said, "If you're going to use my house as a police station I'd like it if you could use some room other than the nursery."

Ives apologized. He and I went downstairs, leaving Tom with Wilson at the telephone. I was thinking that if Sellick had done it then that let Begg Holbrook out. It certainly looked like Sellick, the way he had run out, and with his temperament it could have been, but I thought too that it could have been Begg with his.

"That Stephen Farnum," I asked Ives. "He's a man of good repute, isn't he?"

Ives looked at me.

"In his business he has to be." His voice was a little dry. "Big attorneys don't tell the police that people are at their houses when they're not, Major, not even if they're clients of theirs." He gave a chuckle, a deep, pleasant little chuckle. "You don't like Holbrook, do you?"

I saw it was no use going on about it. I couldn't tell Ives what I had figured out about the Holbrook family. And if Ives was satisfied with his check on the Farnum alibi then I should be too.

I said, "I guess it was Sellick at that."

Ives said, "What kind of man was he at the time you knew him—I mean, how was he in a crisis?"

"Erratic. Yes, he was erratic. He could be more wonderful than anybody, but he could be just the opposite. You never knew."

Wilson came down.

"The Holbrooks will be right over. Guess I'd better get over to the hotel and come back."

Ives nodded.

"And get his picture from the marines." Wilson went out and Ives turned to me. "Do you happen to have any pictures?"

"No," I said. "I never took any pictures through the war."

Ives looked at me.

"That's strange," he said, "especially for a man who likes it enough to stay in."

I don't know why but I began to feel mad at that remark. I was just going to say what I thought of it when Tom came in and Ives asked him if he had any pictures.

Tom said, "Yes, I have some around some place. I'll look them out for you. My assistant says he did not introduce Sellick and Lane and he didn't see them talking together although he remembers she was there that day. I've checked with several people and no one can remember Lane talking with Sellick except that the cop on the gate thinks he remembers seeing them going out together but he's very vague about it. It's pretty well impossible to expect a man to remember a thing like that with so many people going through."

Ives nodded. Tom went over to Elsa's desk in the corner

92

of the room and opened a couple of drawers and hunted through them. After a while he took out a package of letters in a rubber band. He flipped off the elastic and went through the letters and took some snapshots out of one of the envelopes.

"Here are some of Guam I sent Elsa. I think there's one —" He was looking through the pictures and I went over and looked at them over his shoulder and it all came back to me in a rush, those days at Guam, and I thought to myself why did I have to look at those pictures, but somehow I couldn't take my eyes off them. There was a picture of Tom and myself with our arms around each other's shoulders standing beside a tree trunk in the bright white sunlight with the ocean in the background, and lying on the sand beside us was a piece of two-by-four and some bamboo and a couple of empty gasoline cans and a severed head of hibiscus. There was a picture of some planes on a strip with Foraker in the foreground in a pair of swimming trunks standing on his head and putting his tongue out at the camera. There was a picture of seven men in flight jackets snapped as they were standing waiting for something, and I was one of them and I couldn't remember what we were waiting for. There were the seven of us in the group and my eye ran over them all, there was Tom and myself and Joe Carson who was shot down over Tokyo and the Kid from Spain, his name was something ending in owski but no one could ever remember it so we called him that because he looked a little bit like Eddie Cantor, and there were the two Pickerson brothers and George Sellick. You could see George's features very clearly in the picture, it was a good clear picture, and you could see the way he had his head— in anybody else it would have been an arrogant tilt but in George Sellick it was just kind of awkward, it was what you might call his touch-me-not tilt.

Tom gave the picture to Ives, pointing out Sellick.

"There," he said: "You can see him pretty well in this."

93

Ives looked at it a moment and nodded.

"Mind if I keep it a while? I'll have it copied and return it."

Tom said all right and Ives put the picture in his pocket. Tom went to put the other pictures back in the envelope. He put the envelope back among the other envelopes in exactly the same place where it had been before and then he put on the elastic band again and put the package back in the desk and just as he was shutting the desk the front door bell rang and I knew that it would be they, I knew that it would be Janet Holbrook and Begg Holbrook.

Chapter Eleven

SHE HAD ON a black suit and a deep blue sweater that exactly matched the deep blue of her eyes. She saw me directly she came in. He was right beside her. He didn't notice anything, not that there was anything to notice exactly. She didn't know it herself, even. But I knew it, I knew it now in a way that I had not known it before, and all at once it came into my head that maybe all that stuff I had been thinking about him was wishful thinking to free her for me. I thought of what Ives had said about my not liking him, and about Farnum.

It occurred to me now for the first time that if Begg were guilty then Farnum must be too because Farnum had given Begg a perfect alibi, by saying he was at his house and with him at the time of Letty's death, and the idea of the eminent Stephen Farnum's being involved in it was like the idea of President Truman's being involved in it. But I still didn't like him. I still didn't have to like him. He might not be her killer but I wouldn't mind betting he had not objected to his wife's having a twin sister. With any kind of man, come to think of it, it would be quite a situation. But some men would like it and others wouldn't. And I had an idea Begg Holbrook wouldn't object to it. Maybe it was because I didn't like him that I had that idea. He and Janet standing there so close together, a married couple. He had on a suit now and he had shaved and looked presentable for a change. He looked too presentable in fact.

He saw me and didn't like it. I could see he hadn't forgotten my hitting him, he hadn't forgotten it one little bit. But he didn't say anything. He was waiting to see what Ives had to say. He was curious.

Then Elsa came in. I wondered why Elsa had come down but then I saw her eyes go instantly to Janet and I remembered of course Janet is the twin sister of the woman Tom had been out with and I looked at Tom and saw Tom was looking at Janet too and I wondered if he was feeling as startled as I had been, the time I had first set eyes on the twin sister of Letitia. Of course Tom had seen her alive, Letitia, and I had not, so he might notice a different difference from the difference I had noticed. The difference I had noticed was simply that between life and death, but with Tom he would notice the difference between the two living women. I had not thought of that before. Tom would be able to tell whether Janet behaved like Letitia or whether Janet behaved better or worse than Letitia, or lastly Tom would be able to tell whether she, Janet, was precisely the same, no worse, and no better, than Letitia.

Somebody had to introduce people and I saw that there wasn't anybody else to do it except Foraker.

I said "Elsa, this is Mr. and Mrs. Holbrook. Mrs. Marble, Mr. Marble."

They all kind of bowed to each other in the way people do, and then Elsa said, "What about a drink?"

You could see nobody particularly wanted a drink except Begg Holbrook, not that even he seemed to want it really badly but just that he was the type that never refused one. So then Janet changed her mind and said maybe she would have one too, and Tom had to have one to keep them company. Ives refused. He was waiting for all these preliminaries to be over before he carried the ball. His patience stood out, because he must have known that every minute was of value in catching Sellick, but he still had time to let his people get settled and among each other as though there were no officials present before doing any probing. He certainly helped himself in this case by doing it, because it gave time for the latent animosities to grow up all around the room, between Begg Holbrook and me and Begg Holbrook and Tom and between Elsa and Janet too. I could feel it, all the waves of it going sparking and careening round the room, but strangely enough I couldn't feel if there was any feeling coming at me from Janet or not just then, not after that first moment when she had just come into the room. I think maybe she was too tensed up just waiting for Ives, waiting to find out if he had gotten any further in discovering the killer of her twin sister.

Ives said, "Tell me, Mrs. Holbrook, did your sister ever say she had been to the Biltmore Theater in the past week or so? The name of the play is *The Hasty Heart.*"

Janet thought a moment and then looked at Begg and they both looked at each other blankly.

"No," she said, "she never said anything to me about it. She might have been for all I know. We never saw much of her even though she was living with us." She was still thinking hard, you could see she was still thinking hard over the past few weeks, thinking of her sister Letty, of what things she had said and done, trying to remember all those little things that people say and do and which at the time never seem to be important but which in retrospect are those very things that are the milestones of character, the very things that determine another person's ultimate reaction. Janet said slowly, "We were talking about acting one morning, I remember, about a week ago. She was saying something about giving it up and how when you see someone give a good performance it makes you despair of ever doing anything really good yourself. She mentioned some actor's name, but I can't remember it now. She didn't

96

say if she had just seen him or if she was referring to someone she had seen some time ago, but I imagine that probably she had only just seen him." She looked at Ives. "Can
you tell me the names of the people in the cast, and I
might remember if it was one of them?"

Ives, for once, looked helpless.

I said, "I saw it. Could it have been Whitner Bissell?"

She looked at me.

"That was it. Yes, that was the name, Whitner Bissell."

Then they were all looking at me and I saw what I had
done.

I said, "No, I wasn't there with her."

Begg Holbrook said, "Who were you with then?"

I looked at him and I said, "I was there by myself."

Ives checked it. He knew about Sellick and they didn't,
not yet they didn't. He had some more questions for them
first, I could see that.

He said, "Did she go to the movies much?"

Janet shook her head. "Hardly at all nowadays. You
know how bad they've been lately. She saw Henry V twice
I think."

Ives said, "How about the tennis? Do you know if she
went to the recent tennis matches at the Los Angeles
Tennis Club?"

Janet said, "Yes, I know she did that. I was rather surprised because she didn't usually do that."

"Do you know what day or days she went?"

Janet thought a moment.

"I can't remember. She said something about a man who
made an impossible shot with two hands."

Tom said, "That was Segura, the day of the finals." He
looked at Elsa. "Remember?"

Elsa nodded.

"That's right. That was the date of his ticket too," she
told Ives. "Sunday." She looked at Tom again. "They must
have been there, the same day we were."

97

"Could be—I didn't see them, but in a big crowd like that—"

I said, "But there was only the one stub."

Tom said, "You know how it is. People keep their stubs for going in and out. He may have given her hers."

Janet said, "Who? Who are you talking about?"

Ives said, "A man called Sellick—George Sellick." He told them about Sellick, he told them all about how Sellick had been to see Tom and about the novel and his leaving the hotel and everything. They stood there listening intently. They seemed to be going right along with him, until he reached one point. It was when he said something about Letty's having seen Tom and told him that she had turned Sellick down, or rather that she was about to turn him down. And then I happened to be looking at Begg and I saw, quite unmistakably, that this news was a complete surprise to him. He just couldn't help a sudden little reaction of surprise, that sudden slight widening of the pupils and slightest tensing of the person that you can see if you happen to be looking at someone in the actual instant when the reaction occurs and which is gone almost as soon as it happens. I don't think anyone else noticed it, or, if he did, he placed upon it the same connotation that I did. I mean Ives. Now you certainly would expect Ives to notice that kind of thing. It was his job to do so, and there was no one better at his job than Ives. But if he did notice it I knew that he would be putting on it the same answer that would be normal to put on it—simply that Begg Holbrook would be surprised at hearing that Letitia had been definitely planning to turn Sellick down. We had already heard that Tom had advised her to do so, and that in his opinion she was probably going to do so. This further confirmation of the fact was no more than that. Yet to me it seemed strange that Begg should be surprised she had definitely decided to do so and actually said that she was going to do so. You could see he had not expected that.

And there was more to it than just plain surprise. There

98

was hurt there too. There was shock. There was something pretty deep. Although the whole thing was so swift that it took no more than a matter of a second or two, yet I was firmly convinced that Begg Holbrook felt a sense of something very deep indeed.

And then I thought to myself that supposing, supposing he had somehow, despite the Farnum alibi, killed her, killed her out of jealousy at the idea of her being about to marry someone, *not knowing that she had already turned "that someone" down and not giving her a chance to say so,* then that would exactly account for his present reaction. That he had, in other words, killed her to no purpose.

Whether perhaps to cover his reaction or whether because he truly could not bring himself to believe Letitia had made such a definite decision, Begg at that point interrupted Ives to ask how it was that this matter had only just come to light, and why, if such were the case, had Tom not brought it up before.

Tom answered him. He said that he had not brought it up before because he had not thought it made too much difference anyway, for he had thought all along that she would follow his advice, and refuse Sellick, whom she was only marrying to escape some problem of her own. Begg asked him if she had not told him what her problem was, and Tom said no, but that he thought she might have told him later on.

I looked at Janet, again. I knew her eyes were on me. At mention of Letitia's problem Janet's eyes had been drawn to me as though by a magnet, and I knew she wished to see whether I had said anything to Ives about her sister's private tragedy or not, about the "man whom Letitia loved who loved Janet," as she had put it to me in her efforts to conceal Begg's identity. I said, in a speculative kind of way, as we looked at each other, that I wondered what Letitia's problem could have been. I thought that by saying that, it would reassure Janet that I had not said anything against Letitia to Ives. But in a sense the remark was unfortunate, because at that point Elsa (who was I think taking up cudgels for Tom against Begg whom she probably thought provocative in his remarks about Tom's meeting Letitia) said that there probably wasn't any problem at all and that it was a good line to intrigue a nice person like Tom, her director, and get on good terms with him in that way.

Janet, of course, was furious. But she couldn't do much about it. She had already lied to Ives about her ignorance of any problem of Letty's so she couldn't draw back there. Yet at the same time she was put by Elsa in the position of defending her dead twin sister's reputation. The color came into her cheeks and she stood there looking more attractive than ever as she turned on Elsa and told her that that was no way to speak of her dead sister.

Ives cut in. You could see he didn't want to waste any more time. He wanted to catch Sellick. Whether Letitia had had a problem or not was of little concern to him. Having heard what he had about Letitia so far, he probably did not attach too much importance to what she said to Tom, probably agreed with Elsa that it could easily have been a "line" about her problem. Letitia's behavior had not suggested exactly a noble character, and the fact that she was intending to refuse Sellick was to Ives the only important fact as far as he was concerned and he said so. That fact gave Sellick his motivation for killing Letitia, and the fact that he had fled and so far remained in hiding even after the news of her death had been published in the papers strongly suggested that he was the person who killed her.

Tom said that he thought it suggested more than that. He said that he thought that if Sellick had been so much in love with Letitia as to kill her for turning him down then in that case he would not be at all surprised to find Sellick had committed suicide. He said Sellick was the sort of man who would inevitably feel tremendous, overpowering remorse for a deed like that.

Ives was interested. We all were. I did not see how Tom based such an opinion as that, but I realized he had seen

100

Sellick since I had and knew him better. Tom told Ives he based his opinion on Sellick's novel. Ives asked him what it was about and Tom gave him a brief outline of the book. It was the story of a man who had been in a state of mental strain after the war, who had developed a case of bad neurosis necessitating a form of shock treatment electrically administered to the brain, changing the thought paths back to their normal channels and removing the obsession in this way. In Sellick's book the patient did not recover, however, and ended up a suicide, the treatment having failed completely in its effect, thus hastening the disintegration of the personality. The title of the novel, *Pool of Silence*, indicated the last haven of the human spirit, death. He ended his summary with an almost involuntary professional opinion that the story would have to be changed somewhat before making a movie of it.

Ives was noncommittal now, you could see that he was mainly concerned in Sellick's whereabouts and not in this kind of speculation as to his fate, and it was a good thing that Wilson came back just then with the material he had collected from the hotel. He had the papers that had been mentioned, the theater program and the other ticket stubs and the carbon typescript of the novel, but still no clues at all as to where Sellick might have gone. Wilson said that he had been unable to find out anything more and that no one he had questioned had been able to give any hint, since none of them even knew he had been thinking of leaving anyway.

Ives stood thinking a moment, while we all waited around for his next move, waiting to see what the professional was going to do next. He picked up the telephone and called his office to find if there were any reports in yet from his cordon people. While he was waiting for a reply he handed Sellick's picture to the Holbrooks and asked them if they had ever seen him. They both said no, they had not. They had not seen any of Letitia's escorts of late. The reply came back from the police that so far nothing had come up and Ives put down the telephone. I knew he was thinking hard what to do next and I knew he was trying to hide that fact from us. He picked up all the papers that Wilson had brought and started idly riffling through the pages of typescript to cover his thinking. He put the pages down again and his eye fell on the title page and he looked up at Tom.

"What did you say the title of this book was?"

Tom said, "*Pool of Silence.*"

"This one's called *Crystal Lake.*" Ives tapped the pages of typescript. "You sure this is the same book?"

Tom went over and looked at the title page, then at some of the other pages and looked at Ives.

"That's funny," he said. "He changed the title since he brought my copy that first day. I wonder what made him do that. *Crystal Lake.* Same idea of course, not so good thought, I don't think."

Janet said, "Crystal Lake." She turned to Begg. "Why, that's the name of the place you went fishing with Bill Burnette, isn't it, when I went to New York? That beautiful lake in the high mountains that you sent me the pictures of?"

Begg Holbrook nodded. His face seemed to me a little more tense than before and he said, "That's right. Maybe Sellick's been up there too, sort of place any writer or artist would like."

Wilson said to Ives, "It's up in the Mammoth Lakes in the High Sierras north of Bishop. I been fishing there myself once. Sure is beautiful country."

Janet said, "That's a funny thing. That's a funny thing."

We all looked at Janet. She was standing there with the same look on her face as she had had once before when I was with her and she had been thinking about Letitia. That same look of inwardness and studying of herself in a mirror.

She said, "It was Letty who told him about that place. He was an Easterner, wasn't he? He probably hadn't heard

102

of it before. He had only just arrived in California, hadn't he?"

She was looking at Ives, and Ives just nodded, not wanting to break the current of her thoughts. She went on, "Then that's it. He must have shown his book to Letty, and she must have told him about that place, with its Pool of Silence. It looks like that."

Begg said, "But Letty had never been there."

She looked at Begg.

"I know that. But one day I was showing her the pictures you sent me and we were saying what a wonderful place it looked, and I'm quite sure they made a deep impression on her. I know Letty pretty well. We were quite alike in a lot of ways and they made an impression on me, those pictures, and I think they made much more of one on her. I remember noticing it at the time, the way she went and stood by the window afterwards and something she said, I forget exactly what it was, something about life and mountains, what was it now?—I can't remember just what it was, but then when I started to kid her a little about getting in one of her actress moods she said no more about it and I got the impression I had hurt her a little. I told her I was sorry and I was only kidding and she said, 'For goodness' sake, Sis, forget it—it's just the pictures reminded me of a movie I worked in once and there was someone I didn't tell you about,' and so we didn't say any more about it, but I didn't believe that about the movie, I think it was the pictures themselves that brought on one of those moods of hers—she had been getting more and more like that in the past year or so."

Janet stopped talking and there was a silence in the room for a moment as though we all wanted her to go on talking, to go on recapturing that strange scene between the twin sisters. Then Ives said gently, "And you mean, then, that you think Sellick perhaps showed her his book and it brought up the memory of the place she had seen in the

103

pictures and so she told him about the place and he changed the title? Isn't that a little farfetched, don't you think?"

Janet shrugged. "I don't think so, but I can see you might. You see, you didn't know Letty and I did and I think that's just exactly how it might have been if the book of Sellick's is how Mr. Marble described it. And if he was in love with Letty he would certainly have changed the title to the one she told him about—Can't you see, Lieutenant Ives, can't you see a thing like that, how it would be?" Janet was getting impatient with Ives, she was getting very impatient with him for his lack of vision.

It was Ives's turn now to shrug.

"That may be, just as you say," he said, "but my job is to find this man and it doesn't help me to do that."

Janet was looking at him, Janet was looking at him and her eyes were wide and a stray lock of hair had come down across her nose and as she spoke she blew it out of the way without taking time to touch it with her fingers. She was so concentrated upon what she was saying that she probably didn't even know she had blown at her lock of hair or else maybe it was a trick of hers, but that I couldn't tell because I hadn't known her long enough.

She said, "But of course it does help you, of course it does. Can't you see that that's where he is, Crystal Lake, that's where he's gone now?"

Ives looked at her. We all looked at her.

Ives said, "What do you mean?"

"I mean that that's where he's going to kill himself. By the Pool of Silence."

Ives wasn't taking that. He said, "My dear Mrs. Holbrook—"

Janet cut in.

"Then call up and see. Check up and see if he hasn't gone there. Of course he has. Where else would he go after he killed Letty? Where else? He'd go to the place she told him about, the place she intrigued him about, and

104

when he gets there he'll kill himself, he'll be so remorseful he'll kill himself, that's what he'll do, even if he doesn't know it himself yet."

Wilson said, in the silence that followed, "Maybe there's no harm in checking, even if it does sound screwy. I'm getting sick of chasing leads to this guy and finding none. What do you say?"

Ives stood thinking, shrugged and said, "Try it, then. You know the territory, you said?"

Wilson nodded, picked up the telephone. We all stood round, waiting and waiting. Nobody said anything, everybody was watching Wilson and listening to what he said. First he got the long-distance operator and then he got the police in Bishop and they knew nothing. Then he got the Mammoth Lakes district station and they must have told him to hold on pending their inquiries, for he waited a long time before they spoke again and even from where I was standing I could hear the rasping tones of the man at Mammoth when he came on the wire again and said that a man answering the description had packed into the country back of Crystal early that morning. He had gone by himself without guides, taking two animals with him and food for seven days.

Chapter Twelve

IVES had Wilson organize an immediate search party up there for Sellick. He made arrangements to get up there himself by air to Bishop. He told the rest of us that we could consider ourselves free to go and come as we chose providing we were on hand for the inquest, to be held upon his return.

The Holbrooks wanted to go up with him. They wanted to be in at the kill. They wanted to see to it that there should be no suicide. Janet said that nothing would stop her from going up and doing whatever she could to assist in any way she possibly could.

Ives assured her that there was nothing she could do except that she might be able to remember Sellick's voice as being the one she had heard saying good night to Letitia, but for that matter she could do that on their return and that he was going up in his own plane—it seemed that flying was Ives's hobby—which would only take two people.

Begg Holbrook supported Ives, at the same time pleading with him to let him accompany him in the plane. Janet and Begg had quite an argument over the matter, Janet saying that she would go up by herself if Begg went with Ives. Begg shrugged—as long as he could go up at the first opportunity he did not seem interested in whether she came or not. If anything he seemed to prefer that she did not go. This may of course have been in my own imagination only, for certainly his arguments were convincing as to why he should go, that he knew the country well, that Sellick could easily take a great deal of finding and the going could be really rugged, sleeping out and so on, and that since there was not room for both of them in the plane then he was the obvious one of the two to go, whereas she could serve no purpose. Janet remained adamant. She said that they could hire a plane of their own if necessary, and go up she must. She said she didn't feel she could stay behind doing nothing and wondering all that time what they were all doing, whether they were catching the man who killed Letty or not. She admitted she could be of little use—it was simply that she could not bear the idea of sitting by with that man still at large.

Begg comforted her. He said how he understood her feelings perfectly, but it simply was not practical. Ives put a stop to it by saying that he was now going and if Begg wished to come along he could. As they left, Janet still in a high-strung state, I wondered once more about it. I wondered why Begg Holbrook was so anxious to get up there, whether it truly was that he was so deeply concerned as

106

to the capture of Sellick alive, or whether perhaps the suicide angle might not perhaps be playing right into his hands, whether perhaps it might not be exceedingly convenient for him if Sellick were found dead rather than alive, and innocent. And I realized for the first time since I had heard of Sellick's whereabouts that if he were innocent, if he had simply left after Letitia had turned him down and gone up there to solace himself, knowing nothing of her subsequent death, that he might easily know nothing of it because he would very conceivably not have seen a newspaper since he had arrived in that country. And then, if Begg could reach him before Ives, the suicide might be there, a reality, for Ives to find later, a dead body unable to speak, his lips forever sealed. . . .

I borrowed Tom's car and drove around a bit and tried to make up my mind what to do next. I did not want to talk about it to Tom and Elsa because that would have involved betraying Janet's confidence to me as well as making a delicate situation of their own about Letitia even more so. I knew it was no use to tell Ives, certainly not without betraying Janet's confidence that Letty was in love with a man who was in love with her, Janet. If I did that, then I had no means of proving to Ives that that man was Begg Holbrook. Ives would have to question Janet, proving thus to her that I had betrayed her to him.

I found that while I had been thinking I had unconsciously driven down the Holbrooks' street. I was passing the house. Janet came out of the door with a suitcase and walked towards a car parked in the driveway. There was no one in the car and she was alone. I slowed my car and parked it by the curb and got out and walked across the lawn towards her.

She looked up and saw me and was surprised. She stopped and waited for me to come up and I could not tell whether she was pleased or whether she was annoyed or whether she was indifferent, although I could tell that she had been surprised. She was wearing blue jeans now and a colored wool shirt and a mountain jacket and a beret on her head. I said, "Has he gone with Ives?"

She nodded.

"And I'm going right up myself. Did you wish to see me about something?"

"Yes," I said. "I did." I walked up to her and took her suitcase from her before she realized what I was going to do. I started toward my car and she said, "What are you doing?"

"We'll go in Tom's Cadillac. We can do it in six hours if we're lucky. Maybe we can get a plane on the way and save some more time."

She said, "You mean you're proposing to drive me up there?"

I kept on walking towards my car and now she was walking along beside me because she had to. She was still in something of a mood, I could feel that, and I did not want any trouble. I pretended to ignore the fact that we were both walking toward my car and I said, "You must have someone drive you. All that way. Think if you get a flat in the desert or something."

We reached the car and I put the suitcase in the back seat and held the front door open for her to get in.

She was appreciative. I could feel she was appreciative. I could see she had been worried about such a drive by herself and that she welcomed the idea of a protector.

She said, "You know, Major, that's very nice of you. But are you sure you want to do it—isn't it putting you out an awful lot?"

I said, "Why don't you just get in? And stop thinking about things like that. I want to do it. Truly."

She looked at me a moment, and then she got in the car without saying any more. I drove down to Santa Monica and turned right on Wilshire.

When we hit Sepulveda I turned up it and we drove all the way up the pass through the mountains without saying anything. The light was going now and there was quite a sunset. It did not have the grandeur and all of the color of a November sunset, but it was still a California sunset. I felt a strange peace. I felt somehow that for the first time in my life I knew what to do, that I was quite certain about what I was doing and what I wanted to do, and it was a good feeling.

When we reached the top of the pass the sun was almost gone, but the colors were getting better every minute, and the faraway hills on the opposite horizon across the valley were still bathed in a bright sunlight. The valley itself was very lovely, etched out in a sharp evening light that showed up the houses and the series of straight never-ending roads and made them stand right out.

She turned to me then and said, "I'm very grateful to you for not telling those men about what I said. I mean about Letty's trouble."

I looked at her. She was looking very sweet, her beret on the back of her head and that long hair of hers so glossy and well brushed, the ends curling up a little around the nape of her neck.

I said, "I'm glad you're glad."

Then I turned away again and concentrated on the long winding road down the hill. I was driving fast. You can go quite fast down that hill, and I wanted to make as much time as I could. I had an idea that I was going to help save George Sellick's life and I wished to arrive up in Mammoth as soon as I could. But I was careful, I felt inside of me that sureness in my driving that comes perhaps of knowing why you are driving fast.

As I drove along I started to tell her stories, any stories, any stories that came into my head. Stories about the war. Stories about my childhood, the time when my brother was killed in the speedboat. I recalled the whole incident to her vividly and she sat beside me listening very interestedly to it all, how he and I had stolen the boat which belonged to a friend of my father's.

"We had taken a house for the summer on Chesapeake

Bay. It was a late September afternoon and we were both feeling full of devilry that afternoon, like kids are, and we knew we would not be staying there much longer and I said to Danny that it would be a fine idea to slip the Lawrences' boat from its moorings and ride around in it. He liked the idea very much, the kid did, but he was always more cautious than his elder brother and he said did I think the Lawrences would not hear the sound of the motor from their place. I told him that I had heard Mr. Lawrence tell Dad that they were all going back to New York for a couple of days, something about the dentist, and I had thought up the idea of the speedboat at the time because it gave us an opportunity sent by the gods.

"Danny was all for it after that. We climbed aboard and I took the tiller while Danny slipped the moorings from the bows, and I started the motor in the first try. It ran beautifully. I turned and headed out down the bay. She was a big, powerful boat, and I was only a kid of twelve at the time, and I soon realized that I had taken on something harder than I had thought it would be, but I said nothing to Danny about it because I knew the scared feeling would pass in a while when I got used to the handling.

"And pretty soon I was feeling fine and we were singing one of our pirate songs together, Danny sitting further back in the boat now as I put the speed on and the bows came up higher out of the water. I started trying a mild turn and after a while I got bolder and pretty soon I was doing the real thing, sideslipping around at high speed and crossing our own wake. Danny and I were in the middle of the pirate song when it happened. The bouncing caused by crossing our wake at that speed and angle was too much for me and I lost control of the rudder for a second. It was not for more than that but it was long enough for the thing to happen. Danny was jerked clean out of the boat as she slewed, jerked hard into the water. I slowed at once, made my turn and came back to pick him up. I saw him bobbing in the wake, pulled alongside and yelled to him to hang

110

onto the rail till I got to him. He didn't answer. I couldn't make out what had happened. I dived in and got him in my arms. He had broken his neck. He had broken his neck when he first hit the water. He was dead. Danny was dead. Somehow I managed to get him and myself back into the boat, start the motor again and take him home. When I got to the jetty I saw Dad. I don't know if he had seen what had happened way out in the bay there or whether he had heard the sound of the Lawrences' motor or what, but he was standing there waiting on the jetty as I came in. I guess he saw Danny's body right away, for his face went white. I picked Danny up in my arms and held him in my arms while Dad moored the boat, fumbling with the rope because he hardly knew what he was doing. He helped me out of the boat with Danny still in my arms and I looked at Dad and said, 'I killed him, Dad.' Dad never said a word. He just looked back at me for a moment and then put his hand on my shoulder. We took Danny home. My mother was not in when we arrived and in fact I did not see her at all that evening but later when she got back after I had gone to bed I heard her crying, I heard her crying in the night. I did not stir from my room. I did not go to see her. She did not come to see me. In the morning she was not at breakfast and Dad said that she was not feeling well and wanted to see me when I had finished eating. When I went to her room she was in bed. She said, 'Good morning, Jim,' in the way she used to do, and I said, 'Good morning, Mum,' and stood in the doorway waiting. She told me to come in and shut the door. When I had done so she said, 'I want you to know, Jim, that neither Dad nor I will ever feel the slightest blame on you for what happened. I want you to know that, Jim.' I couldn't take it. I had been awake all night and I hadn't cried once since Danny had broken his neck but I couldn't take that. I knelt by her bed and cried my heart out while she stroked my hair and I knew right then that it wasn't true, their not blaming me, and I guess I've known it ever since."

111

Janet did not say anything when I had finished telling her. There was a silence between us. We were driving up Mint Canyon now, we were about halfway through the canyon and the moon was up, and on our right as we sped along the highway I could see the gaunt, black charred hills that had evidently caught fire some time earlier in the year. The black charring made the hills look especially desolate in the moonlight as we drove along. Janet's face was looking a little drawn and white against the black hills and I thought that I saw a tear upon her cheek as I turned my eyes back to the road again and when I looked back at her once more I could see that her shoulders were shaking a little and then I thought to myself, you stupid stupid Foraker, why did you have to go and tell her that story, her of all people, when her sister is lying dead with a broken neck right this minute? And as if in echoing of my own thought she turned to me then and said quietly, "Now I know why you picked Letty up and carried her to safety."

"I never thought of that until this minute. I never even gave it a thought, Janet." I put my right hand over her hands as she sat with them folded in her lap and I said, "I'm sorry. I shouldn't have told you that story."

She said, "I don't know, I think I'm glad you did." She gave my hand a gentle squeeze and then she got out her cigarettes and lit a couple and gave me one and settled back in her seat a little bit.

The car was cruising at around seventy to seventy-five, along the almost empty highway, and we had reached the last cuts in the hills before coming down to the approaches to the desert itself. The night wind was warm from the desert, warm and very dry, not at all like the damp air on the coast that we had by now left far behind us.

Janet started to talk. She started to talk about herself and Letitia, her twin sister, how their lives had always been so bound up one with the other ever since the day they were born until the day when she, Janet, had fallen in love with Begg Holbrook.

112

"I'll never forget that day," she said, "the day I first met Begg. Letty and I were staying with Uncle Stephen in Santa Barbara—we used to stay with him quite a bit after our parents died. That's Stephen Farnum, you know, he isn't really our uncle but we always call him that, he has known us ever since we were little. Well, that evening we were going to a dinner party and Letty wasn't feeling well —she had caught a cold and she was staying in bed, and I wasn't at all keen to go by myself because we always did everything together and we would even feel ill together and perhaps because of that I wasn't feeling too fine myself but I knew it was one of those sympathy things so I went because it had been promised. Begg was there. I suppose we fell for each other right away. And I thought to myself, my goodness, what am I going to say to Letty about this, what am I going to say to Letty when I get back? I thought I'd best keep quiet about it awhile until I was really sure and yet I wanted so much to talk it over with her because it seemed unnatural not to. In fact I decided that she must meet him at once, after all maybe this wasn't really it and anyway Letty should meet him because she might fall for him herself. It was funny that, it was quite strange, the way I wanted Letty to meet him yet also I didn't want Letty to meet him, both at the same time, and when I got home that night she was asleep and I decided not to wake her up and I didn't tell her about Begg, I didn't tell her for several days, by which time Begg and I had seen quite a lot of each other, and then when I did tell Letty I felt as though I had betrayed her. I know it sounds very melodramatic and perhaps it is but that was how I felt. Begg and I were coming into the house across the garden at lunchtime and Letty was up and had come downstairs for the first time since she had been ill because her cold had developed into influenza. But that day she was up and she came across the lawn to meet us and I introduced them to each other. Of course I had told Begg that I had a twin sister so he wasn't particularly surprised or anything, but I hadn't told Letty
113

anything about Begg and naturally it didn't take her long to feel that there was something between us, and I'll never forget the look in her eyes then, the look in her eyes when she realized that I had fallen in love. Of course no one else but me would have noticed it but we were very close together and we always knew what the other was feeling because we always felt the same things together and it was because of that that I also knew that she had fallen in love with Begg too. Naturally Begg didn't know this, and never did, but I always have known it. I don't mean she fell in love with him right away that afternoon although it's always difficult to say about such a thing. Anyway, from then on, there was always that horrible barrier between us. We would both of us try to ignore it but we both knew that it was always there, that the end of our life together had come and that I was going to leave her to get married. Of course we had often discussed such a situation together from the time when we were kids and sometimes we had laughed about it and said that of course we would both have to marry the same man and at other times we would be more serious about it and wonder what it would really be like and the solution we had thought of was that if one of us fell in love the other would have to find someone for herself so that she wouldn't be alone. And that's just what Letty tried to do. But she couldn't. I knew just exactly what was happening and why it was happening. She couldn't fall in love with anyone else because she was in love with Begg. And as for me I couldn't feel properly right about my marriage with Letty feeling that way. Part of me, you see, was always in Letty, and so I suppose that I have never given poor Begg a true chance to be thoroughly happy with me as he had a right to be, and as he should have been and would have been if I hadn't been half of me with Letty. I don't know if you can understand a thing like that, but there it was, and I don't know how to explain it any better than that. And of course it affected Begg. He isn't the same person that he was then, and he knows it

114

and I know it, but maybe Letty had to die, maybe now Begg will be all right again, maybe Letty had to die—for us —maybe—she had to die—"

Janet was sobbing now, she was sobbing her heart out to me, there in the middle of the desert as we drove along.

I slowed the car down a little. Since we had been traveling on the desert floor I had kept the needle at around eighty-five miles because owing to the cool night air I did not consider the danger of a blowout too great, but now I slowed ten miles because I wanted to concentrate on what I was saying and finish it before reaching Mojave which was only ten to fifteen minutes away and I thought that we had better stop there for dinner to set her up.

"You know, Janet," I said, "you know that there is a lot to consider about grief. I know what it is like to lose people and I suppose nowadays we all know it, nowadays is an age of grief for the human race. But she wouldn't want you to feel that way, she wouldn't want it at all. It is much better that you feel happy for her, she is at peace. I'm not much good at saying this kind of thing, I'm afraid, but I'm trying to remember what a padre said to me once when I lost my best friend in New Guinea and he said something to me like that, that we were the ones to feel sorry for because we were still living."

I knew I was talking a whole lot of platitudes but what else I was to say in such a situation I did not know. It had a steadying effect on her and it also served a purpose with me, a purpose of covering up what I was really thinking and working out how best to say. Janet's sobs were less violent now and she was trying to control them altogether. She said, "I know you're right, I know that, but I can tell you this much. I'm not going to rest until we catch that man. I'm not going to rest until he's been executed. And I wish I could execute him myself."

I thought to myself surely it could not have been Begg Holbrook. I thought to myself how can she ever take such a thing if it were Begg Holbrook, and all the time I knew in my heart that somehow it must have been Begg Holbrook and I said, "There is one thing I don't quite understand, and that is if you were in love with your husband then how could any family tie affect that, if you were really strongly in love, I mean?"

She stared at me. She turned in her seat and I glanced at her and I saw that she had started to make up her face and she had not yet finished and she was holding the make-up in her hand halfway to her face as she stared at me in amazement.

"Do you mean to say you don't think I'm in love with him?"

I looked away from her again, I kept my eyes carefully on the highway ahead and I said, "No, Janet, I don't think you are, and I very much doubt if you ever were as completely as you should have been because if you had been then it would have been so much stronger than your love for your sister that that wouldn't have interfered with your love for him. It couldn't have if it had been really 100 per cent."

I knew that it was pretty rough, to say a thing like that to a girl in her position, bereaved. I knew I was taking on a good deal by behaving like that but I felt prepared to take on a good deal because I felt that if my hunch about Holbrook was right then it was better to give her a preparatory slap now so that it would not hit her all of a heap later on. She would be a little more steeled, I felt.

But of course she would not hear of such a thing. She would not hear of it at all. And she got really mad in a good red-blooded way.

She said, "If that isn't the most pompous and conceited statement I've ever heard I'd like to know what is. Just because you've fallen in love with me doesn't mean that I'm not in love with my husband, Major."

I felt my hand shake a little on the wheel.

"Who ever said I had fallen in love with you?"

She laughed, a mean kind of laugh.

116

"If you hadn't you'd hardly be driving me all this way, would you?"

"If you," I said, "if you thought that, then you'd no business to let me drive you and you wouldn't have if you hadn't wanted it."

"Certainly I wanted it. I want to get up there fast and I knew you'd do a good job of looking after me."

"I see. You don't make yourself out very pretty, do you? You mean you take advantage of a man's feelings to better yourself?"

"Major, are you admitting your feelings?"

I said, "There's plenty of reasons for my driving you—" but I couldn't finish the sentence. I couldn't tell her anything yet, about my hunch about Begg. I felt so mad though that I might have come out with something if it hadn't been for the freight train whistling at me just outside Mojave. The road takes a sharp bend right there and you have to slow to twenty miles to cross the tracks and the longest freight train I ever saw was on its way. I saw I would have to stop altogether and wait until it had gone by. I pulled up at the crossing as the first cars were going by and I knew it would mean waiting and I felt mad and my hands were shaking a bit on the wheel and the freight train was making a noise like thunder in my ears and then I saw that she was sitting there and laughing at me and I pulled her across the seat towards me and I took her face in my hands and I kissed her hard right full on her mouth and we stayed like that for a long time, we stayed like that until the sound of the freight train had ceased. And when it had gone we sat apart and she made up her mouth and I started the car again and we drove down the main street of Mojave without saying a word and I parked outside the cafe for dinner and we went into the cafe together.

Chapter Thirteen

THE CAFE was crowded. I found an empty booth, the only one left, in a corner by the window. We sat down and I ordered a couple of highballs, but she shook her head, saying she did not drink. When the waitress had gone I said, "You did this afternoon."

"That was just to keep Begg company."

She took out a cigarette and lit it before I could light it for her. The neon sign in the window was flashing intermittently upon her hair and upon the contours of her face lighting them so that her high cheekbones would stand out and soften, stand out and soften, like that, so that it seemed to add a little to the tension that was inside her. I saw she did not wish to discuss the matter of drinking and I was determined to find out about it.

I lit my own cigarette and I said, "It's because of him you don't do it, isn't it?"

She gave a little frown and said, "I don't know what you mean."

I said, "Janet, look. You can talk with me. You can't go around with all that steam up or you'll bust your boiler."

She said nothing, but there was an involuntary little quirk that came and went quickly at the corners of her mouth. The waitress came with my highball and she said, "All right, I'll change my mind this time."

I gave her my drink and she took a sip of it and leaned back in her seat and then she said, "You know, Jim, it's gotten pretty bad with him lately. Sometimes I wonder what's going to happen."

I said nothing. I said nothing at all, just waited. After a moment she leaned forward again with her elbows on the table and her voice was low. "It isn't just that any more either," she said. "He's started on drugs now too—after you hit him and I got him to bed I found a half-empty bottle of something called chloral hydrate in his pocket. Tell me, Jim, do you know anything about that?"

I said, "Yes, I do. It sends you to sleep. And it's bad."

The waitress came with my drink. I took the highball and ordered two New Yorks, rare. When she had gone I took a long pull at my highball and I said, "What do you suppose is the reason he can't sleep?"

She was looking very troubled again now and she said, "But I told you earlier—it's my fault and I acknowledge it, the way I was about Letty."

I finished my drink and put down the empty glass on the table in front of me and I said, "Don't you think perhaps it's the way he was about Letty?"

She looked at me straight and she said, "What do you mean by that?"

"You know what I mean. You know very well what I mean. I mean he was in love with Letty, that's what I mean."

Her eyes were sparking now.

"What makes you think that?"

The waitress came back and said they were out of steaks but they still had two roast beef. I asked her if it was rare and she said it was not very rare but if I didn't order them we would have to have chicken. I looked at Janet. Her eyes were hard and she just nodded so I ordered the beef and the waitress went away.

I said, "Hasn't it ever entered your head?"

"Of course it hasn't. I've already told you just how everything was. Begg never had a thought like that in his head. The trouble with you is you think too much. First I'm not in love with Begg and then he was in love with Letty. Is there anything else you wish to tell me about my own family?"

The waitress came back with the beef and when she had gone I said, "I'm sorry, Janet, perhaps I shouldn't have said that. I truly don't want you to be upset."

119

"I'm not upset. Just you're making a fool of yourself, that's all. Begg was very fond of Letty, of course, and he knows how much I loved her and that's why he feels so badly about her, but I can assure you that's all there is to it."

I said, "Then I'm sorry I made such a stupid mistake."

I saw she was still put out so I started to eat and then she started to eat too and we did not talk any more until we had finished. The juke box was playing across the room and when it stopped playing I went over and put in a quarter and pressed five buttons and came back and finished my coffee and got the check. Janet was sitting over her coffee and smoking a cigarette and I wondered what she was thinking about.

I said, "Perhaps we'd better get going and not lose more time than we can help."

She nodded and finished her coffee and stubbed out her cigarette. When we were in the car again and we had started traveling and had left Mojave behind us for the long miles through the desert she said, "I was thinking about the last time I saw Letty, remembering it all. To think it was only yesterday, all that has happened since. We had lunch together and Begg was in Santa Barbara and I wanted to go to the beach and asked her to go with me but she said no, she had a date at three o'clock, so I went with a friend instead. I was trying to remember how we said good-by, I was trying to remember what I said and what she said but it was just quite casual of course, something like, have a good time. I know I was careful not to say anything much about the date because once before, the night I was closing the living-room window, I heard her say good night to him and she came in and told us she was going to be married. When we asked her to tell us his name she said no she wouldn't tell us yet, not until she was quite sure."

I said, "I don't quite get that. If she wasn't sure how could she get engaged?"

120

"Letty was very confused, the poor baby. She was very confused."

I said, "Did she say she wasn't sure in front of Begg or just to you?"

Janet looked across at me. I could see out of the tail of my eye that she was looking across at me but I didn't look at her, I just kept my eyes on the highway ahead because there was a string of headlights coming towards us and one of them would not dim his lights down. I would flash with my dimmer at him and then one of the others who was already dimmed would flash his brights back at me and so it went on as Janet was answering me.

"What makes you ask that?" she said.

I passed the front two cars and came to the one with brights on and turned mine on full once again. His lights went out altogether for a second and then came on full again. He didn't have any dim lights at all. I dimmed mine for him and concentrated on the road until I had passed him and turned my brights on again.

I said, "I'm sorry, I was concentrating. What were we saying?"

"You asked me if she told Begg she wasn't sure. As a matter of fact she didn't, she told me upstairs later. She just stopped by the living room on her way up and said she was engaged and when we asked his name she said she would tell us when she introduced him because she didn't want us to form any pictures of him in our minds before we met him. Later, upstairs, when we were alone together I asked her again to tell me more about him and she told me she wasn't quite sure yet but she thought she was and so I said no more about it. What made you ask about that?"

"I don't know," I said. Then I said, "Perhaps I was thinking that she would not want Begg to know his name so that he could not go and tell him about Letty and himself and mess things up that way."

Janet said, "Are you on that tack again? I've told you there wasn't anything between them."

"But you did say you knew she loved Begg."

"Begg didn't know that."

"That's right, I forgot." I shifted gears down to second to wait for a truck that was slowed right down. We were on a grade twisting among the red rocks and I could not see far enough ahead to pass him, so I had to wait my chance.

I said, "Sellick must have moved fast to get up to Mammoth when he did, if he was with Letty around three o'clock. We know he doesn't have a car and busses take ten hours, at least. And there aren't many busses on this route, probably only two a day I should think. And they go from downtown, you can bet on that. So Sellick would have had to go downtown first, he would have had to do some shopping if he was intending to pack in. Then he would have had to get a bus because there are no trains for that country. And he probably had to wait for the bus for some time."

Janet said, "What do you mean? Do you mean it was somebody else?"

"No, he could have done it. Probably there's an evening bus and he was on that. I suppose it would always be possible to check. The driver or maybe some of the passengers would remember on a long drive like that. You know how those bus trips are, people get to know people and so on."

"What are you trying to say? That it wasn't he who killed Letty?" She was all tensed up again, sitting up in her seat and trying to read my face by the light of the dashboard. I sensed for sure, the way you can sometimes, that she wasn't anywhere near ready to take anything like that about Begg. I sensed it for sure.

So I said, "It couldn't have been anybody else, you wouldn't think. No, I was just working things out in my own mind how he went about it all afterwards, the bus and so on. Maybe he got a ride up, hitch-hiked. I expect he

122

was on the evening bus though, I imagine there *is* an evening bus."

Janet said nothing for a moment. I passed the truck and got into the clear road ahead again and waited for her to speak. She was still tensed up but not quite so much as she had been.

She said, "But it *must* have been him because of everything. He must have got up there somehow, but that doesn't matter how." She did not sound too sure. But then she remembered something. "Of course, his voice. You'd forgotten that I shall be able to tell if it was his voice or not. And I'm sure it must have been."

I said, "That's right, you will, won't you?" I had the car back to its usual speed again now and we were rolling the desert miles up steadily, but there was still going to be a long drive through the night hours. I looked at her and she was sitting back in the corner again now and I said, "Why don't you curl up there or in the back seat and try and get some sleep. You'll be much more efficient that way when you arrive."

She said, "I believe I will at that. I'll just curl up here. If I put my foot in your ribs wake me up, and I'll go in the back."

"You won't be in my way."

I leaned across her and pressed down the lock on her door so as not to take any chances. As I leaned across, my hand accidentally touched hers, and she did not react and I did not react and neither of us said anything about it, and then she curled up on the seat and put her beret on the arm rest and put her head on it and went to sleep. I could not tell whether she was asleep or not but I presumed she was since she did not talk any more as I drove along through the night. I could see the High Sierras now upon my left and the mountains looked very big in the desert moonlight.

As I drove on and on I thought how alike were the desert and the sea, and memories of flight returned to me, the

123

sensations and the thoughts which had occupied me on those days in the Pacific, days and nights of sometimes solitary flight over that great sea, not the part of my mind that was concentrated upon my instruments and upon the never-ceasing watch for that speck on the horizon that would be death if unobserved while it was still a speck, but the other part of my mind which would work even while my head was continually turning, turning, while my eyes were probing the entire circle of horizon, probing upwards and downwards as well as in a circle so that they continually examined the total globe of my always changing sky. The other part of my mind, during those periods of waiting for some action, would be occupied with memories of peace at home, with hopes and fears of perhaps some future peace that I might see if I always saw the speck in time, if my luck should hold, if a hundred things to one that were against me were not against me, if I were one of the ones and not one of the hundreds.

Then, as now, I knew that there was an enemy ahead, standing between me and the memories of my future wife. Often in those days I had had memories of my future wife, as though the future were the past, in case there was to be no future. And, traveling at high speed through those globes of sky, the future and the present and past would merge themselves so that they were one, as in a dream, and it would be as easily possible to remember the future as the past since both were always present. And I remembered quite clearly now, suddenly as though I had been struck by much electricity, that once I had remembered Janet's face. Janet's face, Letitia's face, which was it though, for they were both the same and one was dead? Still I could not tell who was my enemy ahead, which of those two men had killed Letitia, whether it was Janet's present husband so that I could be her future one, or whether it was Sellick, so that I should have been Letitia's. Or I might simply have been remembering that I was going to see Letitia's dead face.

124

My thoughts were losing their coherence, yet I had a sensation of becoming more keyed up. Looking at the instruments on my dashboard I saw that the gas was running low. Ahead I saw the neons of a service station and I started to slow down. Beside me, Janet woke up.

She stirred a little on the seat at the change of rhythm of the car, and as I glanced at her she looked up to see what was going on.

I said, "I'm stopping for gas. You can keep right on sleeping."

She yawned and stretched and sat up and said, "I'll get a little fresh air while we stop." She took out her comb and combed her hair and looked at her face in the mirror and sighed at it as we drew up.

I said, "It isn't bad as all that, sleepyhead."

The boy came out of the station and I got out and went to meet him out of earshot. He had sandy hair and freckles and a disarming smile and he said, "Hullo, Major, you still at it, huh?"

I said, "I've an idea. I'm going to follow your example any day now." I didn't resent it any more. Something had changed me in the past twenty-four hours so I didn't resent cracks about still being in any more. I said, "You know anything about the busses that run by here from L. A. to Mammoth, how many there are and when they run?"

"Afraid I don't," he said. "They don't stop here. Wish they did. Shall I fill the tank?"

"Please. Where's the telephone?"

"Right there, on the right as you go in the inner door."

"Thanks."

I saw it would be out of sight of the car, and even if she got out she would not come by there. I went in to the station and through and found the phone and got the long-distance operator.

"I want the Greyhound Bus Company in downtown Los Angeles."

"One moment, please."

125

I waited while she got to Los Angeles and found the number. While I was waiting I got out my change and laid it out ready to put in the machine. I heard her get the Los Angeles operator who said the number was TRinity 9781. Then the line went dead awhile and then her voice came through again.

"Greyhound Bus Company, one moment please. That will be seventy cents for the first three minutes, sir."

I put in two quarters and two dimes.

"Go ahead please."

I said, "I want some information please. I want the schedules for the busses leaving you for Mammoth Lakes, California, time of departure and arrival."

"One moment please."

I waited. After a while I got it.

"Bus for Mammoth departs 9:30 A.M., arrives Mammoth 7:30 P.M. The other two only run to Rock Creek, half-hour difference. Depart 2:30 P.M., arrive Rock Creek 12:01 midnight. The third bus leaves Los Angeles 7:45 P.M., arrives Rock Creek 5:15 A.M. Fare is $7.30 single and $12.45 return. Is that the information you required, sir?"

I wrote it all down as it was said.

I said, "Is there any way of checking whether a certain passenger was on one of your three busses Thursday? I mean if I gave you the name or description could you tell me?"

"I'm afraid that would not be possible at this time of night, sir. If you care to leave the name and description we might be able to do that, you just can't tell."

"Thank you, that's all then."

I hung up the receiver and put the balance of the change back in my pocket and I thought that since Sellick had been seen in the hotel in Beverly Hills at some time between 9:30 and 10:00 A.M., then he couldn't possibly have been on the morning bus. If, as I expected, he had gone on the 2.30 P.M. bus then he could not have killed her, since she did not die at the earliest before 3:00 P.M. and more probably after that, in Beverly Hills too. That meant that if he

had arrived at Rock Creek at 12:01 midnight he was innocent. The only bus he could possibly have taken if he killed
her was the one leaving Los Angeles at 7:45 P.M. and
reaching Rock Creek at 5:15 A.M. If he had arrived at Rock
Creek at 5:15 A.M., he could have done it, he probably had
done it in fact. So now I had it. If he arrived at midnight he
was innocent. If he arrived at 5:15 A.M., he was probably
guilty. I reached the car and paid the boy for the gas. Janet
was still away so I got in and waited for her. I could see the
boy was wanting to talk about the war with me while we
waited for Janet so I said, "How long will it take to get to
Rock Creek from here, that's a little this side of Mammoth?"

"In that car, let's see, Mammoth if you really travel, you
could make it around two hours and a half I guess."

Janet came back and I opened the door for her.

I said, "Thanks, that's about what I figured."

"Stop in on your way back."

"You bet." I swung the door closed as she got in and
started off again.

Janet said, "The air has really woken me up, it's just wonderful. Who were you telephoning to?"

"Telephone? Oh, that, I was trying to get through to
Mammoth to get some reservations but the line was busy."

"That line's always busy. It's a party line up there and all
the places around are on it."

"I thought you'd never been up there."

"I haven't, but when Begg was up there fishing last July
and I was in New York we had an arrangement that he call
me long distance every evening at seven. Nearly every night
we'd have to wait ages and even when he did get through
there would be people always cutting in to see if the line was
clear." She lit a cigarette and said, "We'd best try the
Marmazon first, that's where he and Bill Burnette stayed.
Begg's probably there now again."

I said, "I'd like a cigarette too, and then it's your turn
to tell me some stories now you're awake again."

She gave me a cigarette and said, "Stories—what kind of stories do you like?"

"Oh, about your childhood or something. Tell me about your Uncle Stephen. You've known him for years, haven't you? He's supposed to be quite a character."

"Uncle Stephen? Hes not really our uncle, you know."

"Yes, you told me. He was a friend of your family's, wasn't he?"

"He and Dad knew each other from way back, they were at Harvard together and became friends there." She took a pull at her cigarette and I knew she was thinking about her dad. "It's funny, how different those two were, you'd never have thought they would be friends, they were just the opposite from each other, Dad was so gay and kind of irresponsible—I don't mean he was really irresponsible but he kind of put on an act of being it, rather like you in fact —" She broke off and looked at me quickly as I looked at her and I couldn't see her face properly in the dark car lit only by the dashlights and she couldn't see mine properly either I suppose but I thought I knew what her expression was, I thought I knew, and I thought maybe I should stop the car and kiss her again and then I thought it would take too much time to stop and start again when we were racing to save Sellick, as I was sure we were doing, so I just laughed and said, "Thank you. I've been called it before but never so nicely."

She laughed and said, "So it's true, is it?" She went on before I could answer, "Anyway Dad was like that, and Uncle Stephen was always so serious and careful about everything though maybe part of that was due to his carrying the torch for Mum—they both fell in love with her, you know. In fact Mum met Uncle Stephen first and they were, oh I don't know, mind you, but from little things Mum dropped throughout the years I've often thought she would have married him if she hadn't met Dad, but then she said she fell in love with him the first moment she set eyes on him and Uncle Stephen knew he was a dead duck from then

128

on and bowed out. But he was very sweet about it and stayed friends with them both though he didn't see us too often, he worked so hard, I've often thought one reason he did so well was to escape from the torch he carried for Mum." She fell silent a moment and then she went on, "We didn't see a great deal of him but he would always spend Christmas with us and he was wonderful to Letty and me. He never forgot our birthday and then, when Mum and Dad were killed, he took charge of us. He was as hurt as we were, I guess."

She fell silent again and I said, "How long ago was that?"

"Nineteen forty-two—Dad went to London on the air board and Mum went to be there for a while and they got a direct hit on their house."

I thought, and now Letty. I just didn't know what to say, so I said nothing at all and I think she liked that. After a while she went on again, "I don't think Uncle Stephen has ever been the same since. He's changed quite a bit, gotten a lot older, sits longer over his meals, has more than one liqueur after lunch—in fact, especially since I got married and Letty decided to act and we all moved away, he hardly seems to have very much to live for. He has his work but he doesn't do too much of that any more. He must have been quite a bit older than Dad even though they were at Harvard together, I guess. But either Letty or Begg and I would try to visit him every week end. We tried having him stay with us in Beverly but it didn't work out—he just isn't happy away from his own house."

"He must have been terribly upset about Letty."

"He was, very. He wanted to come right over but he wasn't feeling well enough. I didn't know he was sick or I wouldn't have told him then. Begg said he was all right at lunch."

"What was the matter with him?"

"To tell the truth I didn't ask, I was just thinking about Letty."

"How come you weren't lunching with him too?"

"Begg wanted to talk business and I'd only just seen him anyway so I went to the beach." She looked at me, I could feel her watching me from the corner. She said, "Are you trying to find out something?"

I said, "Hell, no, honey. I was just interested in you and your family, that's all. Can you see the name of this town we're coming to? I guess it's Lone Pine."

She looked out her side to watch for the sign as I slowed for the speed limit.

"That's right, it is."

"We won't be too long now. You've time for another nap if you want. I'm going to stop at Rock Creek to fill the tank because I know what happens when you get up in the mountains, the price of gas goes up too and Rock Creek's probably the least cheap place."

"Sure you wouldn't care for me to drive a bit?"

"No, thanks. I'm not much good at being driven."

She settled down in her corner again, curled on the seat. She said, "Maybe somebody will tame you one of these days."

"You never can tell."

She did not answer. She must have gone to sleep almost instantly. I could feel waves of sleep coming over me too and I knew I was taking a chance in driving on and on but there was just no other way around the matter. I had to get to Rock Creek, and then on up to Mammoth. I couldn't turn the radio on because of waking her. I started whistling to myself under my breath. I whistled under my breath all the way from there to Rock Creek, every tune that I could remember hearing since I had been born. I whistled for the best part of two hours.

Chapter Fourteen

WHEN I got to Rock Creek it was way after midnight, it must have been around one o'clock in the morning. There was one man on duty at the station and I pulled in there and got out to talk with him before Janet woke up. I had taken a lot of trouble in slowing down so that the rhythm would not change more than I could help and she was still sleeping dead away when I stopped. She looked very cute with her hair all tumbled around and that little nose. I closed the door very gently as I got out and the man came to meet me. He was around forty-five, bald as a coot too. He had keen responsible eyes and he looked as though he had a good memory.

I said, "A friend of mine came up here by bus Thursday night and I can't find him without knowing which bus he was on, the twelve-o-one midnight or the five-fifteen in the morning. I wonder if you could help me."

He said, "Afraid I wasn't on duty Thursday night at midnight. I was here for the five-fifteen though. What does he look like?"

"He's tall and thin and dark with gray eyes. Age around thirty-two, -three. Serious looking. He would have had fishing and camping equipment with him because he was going to pack in at Mammoth."

His eyes got thoughtful.

"Fisherman. They was two—three fishermen, but I don't remember one looked like you say. And they stopped right here anyway, they didn't go on to Mammoth. But could be I missed him, bus was pretty full. Shall I fill the tank?"

"Thanks. Would there be anyone around who was here for the midnight bus?"

"You couldn't talk with him now, Major. He'd just about cut your throat or his wife would if you tried awaking him. In the morning he'll be here, comes on at noon I think it is."

"Okay, thanks a lot."

"Sorry I couldn't help you any. That's three dollars seventy-five."

"Thank you. Good night."

"Good night."

I got in and started up and drove off without waiting to

131

check the oil and water. She was still asleep as I drove on up the mountain road. I didn't feel sleepy any more, not now I didn't. I was beginning to feel pretty certain Sellick had not been on the five-fifteen. I was beginning to feel pretty certain Sellick had been on the midnight. That made it Begg. Unless I was crazy. But how?

Halfway up the hill she stirred. The air probably did it. It was a good thing anyway, gave her time to come to properly before we got in.

I said, "Hullo, there. We're almost in."

"Rock Creek?" she asked, her voice still crinkly with sleep.

"Mammoth. You didn't wake at Rock Creek."

"Oh."

She started to freshen herself up.

I said, "This Marmazon. What kind of a place is it?"

"I don't know. But you can bet it's one of the best or Begg wouldn't have stayed there."

"I heard it wasn't too good. The man at Rock Creek told me it had gone off a lot lately. Why don't we try another place first?"

"If you don't mind let's go to the Marmazon. I've an idea Begg will be there. And you want to see the lieutenant, don't you?"

"Not specially. And anyway they may be gone by now. If they flew into Bishop early last evening they may have gone right off in the mountains by now." I saw she was beginning to wonder so I said, "Okay, we'll go to the Marmazon first."

I came on it sooner than I expected. It was about the first one as you got up there. It was a big log business with Marmazon spread in blue neon right across. It looked comfortable and modern.

I pulled in to the front porch and stopped my motor. Janet got out. I got out. We walked up the steps to the lobby together. The lobby was in half-light. There was no one at the desk. We walked up to the desk together and I

132

pressed the bell. We waited. We waited for perhaps two minutes and lit cigarettes. We didn't say anything. A man came down the hall. As he came nearer and you could see him properly by the desk light you could see he was around fifty or perhaps a little less. He had a nice expression on his face, considering he had been woken up, but at the same time it was his job to have a nice expression on his face. But as he got closer and looked at Janet his expression changed into one of real pleasure and surprise and this time you could see he really meant it.

He held out his hand to her and he said, "Well, hullo there, Mrs. Holbrook. How nice to see you again. Your husband never told me you were coming too, I expect he forgot to mention it. You've got the same room you had last July. He's there now, if you care to go right along?"

Janet was staring at him. She was staring and staring at him, and now her face was dead white. It couldn't ever ever have gotten any whiter than it went then. And then she slid to the floor at our feet.

I bent down and picked her up and carried her to the davenport across the vestibule. The little man was looking very puzzled. I said, "It's the mountain air. We came up too fast. Got any brandy?"

"Brandy? I guess so, I'll see." He went off, still puzzled and brought a bottle and a spoon from the next room. I poured some brandy in the spoon and held it to her lips and trickled it into her mouth. The little man said, "I'll go and tell her husband."

I said, "Not now. I'll see him later."

"But she's sick, he should be here."

She was beginning to stir, the color was beginning to come back to her cheeks. The little man was starting to go down the hallway to get Begg Holbrook. I left her for a moment and caught up with him and stopped him with my hand on his sleeve. I said, "Look, I don't want him brought here now or told she is here."

He looked at me and he looked at her and back again

133

at me and he said, "I can't believe it—there was one couple that were happy together if ever there was one." He shrugged and his eyes went listless and bitter and indifferent and he said, "After that I give up. They were the happiest couple I ever saw."

Janet's eyes were open now and she heard what he said. I could see she had heard what he said.

She said, "I think I'd like to go to my room, if you've got one vacant. I won't disturb my husband tonight."

The little man shrugged and went to the desk. I signed for the rooms and got the keys and he showed us where the rooms were. They were down the other end of the hallway from Holbrook's. All the time I had been thinking that he might come out and see us but he didn't, he was evidently fast asleep. I didn't want Janet and him to meet while she was like this. You could see she was still in a state of shock.

I got her suitcase from the car and took it to her room. When I got back she was lying on the bed staring up at the ceiling, so still, you would have thought she was asleep if it had not been for her eyes being wide open. She did not speak or say anything or move when I came back. I shut the door and went and sat on a little chair by the bed and took her hand. It was ice cold. I got up and took off her shoes and got the blankets from the foot of the bed and put them over her and tucked them in around her and turned out the top light and left the little light burning on the side table. She did not move or say anything. I sat down again beside her and waited. I was beginning to wonder if she realized that I was there or not when her head turned toward me and I saw her eyes were full with tears and when she spoke her voice sounded very far away and foreign to her.

"Letty," she said. "How could she have done that to me?"

I said, "Provocation. In other words, Begg took advantage of the situation."

134

She was still staring in front of her.

"Those pictures," she said. "No wonder she was upset by those pictures."

I said, "I'm going to leave you to sleep now. Do you think you can sleep?"

It wasn't any use. She did not even hear me. She was still thinking about her sister's betrayal of her, not her husband's, but her sister's. She lay there, staring, staring. All at once she half sat up, brushed the hair from her face.

"Now I see. Now I see. How right you were about them. If it hadn't been for me, she wouldn't have died. She wouldn't have gotten in trouble. It should have been her and Begg instead of me and Begg."

I said, "Stop that, Janet. It's no use talking like that, it's wrong even to think like that. Life isn't an if, life's life, what happens happens and to heck with it. Who do you think you are to carry on like that, you're just one small person out of two thousand million people on this globe and most of the others are starving and ill and in pain. Now you're darn well going to sleep and shut up. I'm going to stay here until you go to sleep."

The light from the side table caught her hair, it was a soft pale orange light and it caught her hair and it caught the contours of her face and it shone also on her throat. She was still wearing her wool shirt open at the neck without any scarf or necklace or any form of adornment and the small circle of orange light from the tilted lamp shade framed her head and neck in its color so that she looked like a stained-glass madonna.

She said, "No wonder Begg wants to kill him. And if he doesn't kill him, I'll do it myself."

I stared at her.

I said, "What makes you think Begg wants to kill him?"

"Because he was in love with Letty. I see it now. That's why he wanted to come on ahead of me, that's why he looked like he did, that funny tight look that comes over

135

his face sometimes—" she broke off suddenly as a thought came to her mind. She said slowly, "That funny tight look —" she raised her hand to her mouth and looked at me and through me and she said, "I can't take it, half those times, half those times he was with me he was thinking about her, wishing I was her, I must go to him at once, I must make sure for myself, I must look in his eyes and see it—" She was starting to get up, her voice was increasing in its note of hysteria.

I slapped her face.

She stayed quite still for a moment, looking at me in astonishment. Then she began to cry. I said, "I'm sorry, Janet, I had to do it."

"The hell you did. You let me up at once. I'm going to see Begg right this minute."

I said, "Listen, Janet. There's something more you've got to understand. I don't believe Sellick was on the evening bus. I think he left town before Letty died. I think she turned him down the evening before. I think the afternoon date she had was with someone else. I didn't want you to know yet but you're forcing me to tell you."

"What do you mean?' She stared at me. "What do you mean?"

"I'm morally certain Begg killed Letty."

She stared and stared.

Then she said, "You really are crazy, aren't you."

"No, I'm not—he was insanely jealous of her marrying Sellick."

Janet sat up. She was not crying any longer now. She had not troubled to wipe the tears from her cheeks. The line of her lips and her chin was firm and taut and determined.

"She wasn't going to marry Sellick, you fool. And Begg was in Santa Barbara anyway. I've had enough of your romantic nonsense for one evening. Get out of my way."

I put my hands on her arms, holding each arm just below the elbow.

"Begg didn't know she decided against Sellick. I was

136

watching his face when it came up about her intending to turn him down. He was badly shaken."

"But he was with Uncle Stephen. Uncle Stephen wouldn't lie about a thing like that."

"Perhaps Begg found some way of slipping in to Beverly and back without his knowing. That's what I want to telephone and find out about. Please, Janet, will you stay here while I do that? Then, if I'm wrong, you can see Begg. But if I'm right, can't you see how dangerous it is for you to see him?"

But she would not listen. She would not listen at all.

She said, "I'm going to see Begg, and you can't stop me."

I twisted her around and got both her arms behind her back while she kicked and threshed about on the bed. I got both her arms together and got hold of them in my left as she began to shout and I quickly got out my handkerchief with my right hand and stuffed it in her mouth and stifled the scream before it had started. I looked around for something to tie the gag in with. Her suitcase was lying half open by my feet and I kicked it over so that all the clothes came out and spilled all over the floor, skirts, blouses, underclothes, and what I was looking for, two pairs of silk stockings. I got one of the stockings close to me on the floor by dragging at it with my foot. Then I let go the gag for a second with my right hand and bent down and got the stocking before she knew what I was doing. The gag was still firm in her mouth. I twisted the stocking around it as best I could with one hand and around her head and tied it with my right hand and with my teeth. Then I took off my belt and tied it around her arms tight and then around the rail of the bed and buckled it firm. I tied her ankles with another stocking. I left her lying like that on the bed and went out. Her eyes followed me out, sparking blue fire. I slipped out of the room and made my way to the desk and found the telephone booth over against the wall. The little man heard me from his cubbyhole place and came shuffling out and looked at me.

"Oh, it's you," he said.

I said, "Yes, it's me. The Inspector Lieutenant who came with Mr. Holbrook—which room's he in? It's urgent."

Now I had gotten him all puzzled again. You could see he couldn't figure how Janet and I could have known that her husband was here. He gave it up.

He said, "He's in the room next door."

"Show me. I've got to talk with him."

"You can't right now. He's out."

"Where's he gone?"

"Mammoth Pack Station, he said. He said he'd be back later. He's been gone a long time now."

"Did Mr. Holbrook go too?"

"No, he's asleep in his room."

"Okay, thanks."

I made my way to the telephone booth and went in and read the notice on the wall which said first to pick up the receiver and make sure no one else was using the line and then replace the receiver and give one long ring for the operator and the number of this telephone was Marmazon.

I picked up the receiver and there was no one on the line so I put it back and gave a long ring and listened for the operator. After about thirty seconds she came on the wire and asked what number I wanted.

"I want long distance, please, operator."

"One moment please."

I waited. I heard a click on the line.

"Long distance. Number please."

"I wish to speak with Mr. Stephen Farnum of Santa Barbara, California."

"I'm afraid I can't hear you very well. Can you speak a little louder please?"

"I want Mr. Stephen Farnum of Santa Barbara, California."

"Stephen Farnum, Santa Barbara. Who is calling please?"

"Mr. Holbrook."

138

"Will you speak with anyone else at that number, Mr. Holbrook?"

"No, just Mr. Farnum."

"Thank you. What is your number please?"

"Marmazon."

"Thank you. One moment please."

A man's voice said, "What's the idea, Foraker?"

"Ives, is that you?"

"Yes. What are you doing?"

"Are you at the pack station?"

"Yes."

"I've been wanting to get in touch with you. Did you find out what time Sellick got to the pack station?"

"He packed in at three in the morning."

"Then he didn't do it, Ives. He must have come on the midnight bus which leaves downtown before she was killed in Beverly."

"I know it. He did come on it. I've just been checking. Why are you calling Farnum?"

"To find out why he's giving Holbrook an alibi. If it wasn't Sellick it must have been Holbrook."

"Correct. I've found out some things too. You're doing quite well, Major, but I wish you'd check with me before acting on your own as you're doing now."

"Shall I cancel the call?"

"It was never put through. I called Farnum just this moment myself. I made him really talk."

"You did? What happened?"

"Holbrook was there all right. Farnum and he tried some new South American liqueur Holbrook had brought him. It must have contained wood alcohol because they both passed out cold from one-thirty to five-thirty when Farnum came to and revived Holbrook. The old man's still feeling plenty ashamed of himself."

"Ives, I've got it."

"What?"

"That was chloral hydrate, not wood alcohol."

"Chloral hydrate?"

"Holbrook's wife found a used bottle of it in his pocket that evening. He must have slipped Farnum a mickey, got his Cadillac, made it in to Beverly and back, yes he could well have done it in the time by taking chances, then given himself a mild dose of the stuff so he was out when Farnum came to. He knew Farnum wouldn't talk about it. And he darn near got away with the alibi."

"That's it then. Listen, I'll be right back. Is he still asleep?"

"Yes."

"See he doesn't slip out before I get back. He's liable to be after Sellick as soon as the cloud lifts on the Crystal trail."

"I'll watch him."

Ives hung up. I put the receiver down and went out into the hallway to get the gun from the glove compartment of the car. The little man wasn't in sight so he must have gone back to his cubbyhole. I went by the corridor that led to Janet's room and there was some light streaming out into the corridor, cutting across it from one of the rooms where somebody had left his door open with the room lights on. It looked to me like Janet's own door but I couldn't be sure without going down the corridor to look. Maybe it was my own room that was next door but I hadn't been in there yet and I had not seen the little man go in either.

I went down the corridor. It was Janet's room all right. The room was empty. And her shoes, which I had taken off and put down by the foot of the bed, were gone.

I raced for Begg Holbrook's room on the other side of the hotel. Number five. I had seen it in the register when I was signing. Number five. The numbers went fifteen, thirteen, eleven, nine, seven, five. The door was closed. I turned the handle, as quickly and as quietly as I could. The door swung open. The room was in darkness. I clicked on the light and there was nobody there. Nobody at all. The bed had been slept in and the covers were left all anyhow. There was a

140

holdall and a suitcase lying open with some of his clothes lying around, city clothes that he had traveled up in probably. And also lying on the floor was an empty, newly opened box of rifle shells, thirty-thirty, steel jacket, the kind you use for deer hunting.

The little man was standing in the doorway.

He said, "What do you think you're doing?"

I took him by the arms and it was all that I could do not to shake him. I said, "Quick, what happened to Mrs. Holbrook? Did she meet him?"

He looked at me.

I said, "Look, this is a serious, police matter. There's a killing involved. And if you don't talk fast there may be another, there may be two more in fact."

He said slowly, "Well, you seem genuine enough. Maybe I better tell you. Mr. Holbrook left while you were in the phone booth. Had a Springfield with him, said he was going deer hunting to Crystal. Just after he left she came by to see him. She asked me where he'd gone and I told her. I guess she followed him, I told her which way the trail was but I don't know if either one of them can get along it yet. If the fog's lifted they can, if not they'll have to wait awhile."

"Thanks. You got a rifle?"

"Well, I—"

"Quick, man, where is it?"

He looked at me.

"Okay," he said, "I'll get it for you."

He went down the hall, shuffling along in the way he did, and I thought he would never get there at the pace he went. Halfway along he started shaking his head.

"I dunno why I should be doing this," he said. "I don't at all know why I should be doing this." He looked up at me, pondering. "How'm I to know you are on the level about all this? Maybe I better wait till the inspector gits

I took a hold on myself. I looked back at him very calmly back."

and in an earnest manner that I sensed he would appreciate.

I said, "I can well understand your outlook. If I were in your boots I would feel the same myself. It's up to you to decide. I can't force you. But there's one thing you've forgotten."

"What's that, mister? What have I forgotten?"

"Why do you think the inspector is here at all if it isn't a police matter?"

He thought about that for a while and then he gave his little shrug. He said, "I guess so." He thought a little more and then he said again, "I guess so." Then he started off again down the hall. He turned in at his cubbyhole place and went through into a bed-sitting-room and I followed him in. There was a rack on the wall and there was a Mannlicher on the rack. He reached up and got it down and handed it to me. I opened the breach and saw it was unloaded and saw the barrel was clean. He was getting some shells from a box in his table drawer. He held out a handful.

"These be plenty?" he asked.

I took the shells and looked them over. They were all right, Peters high speed, thirty-thirty.

I said, "That'll be fine, thanks."

I loaded the rifle and put the remaining shells in my pocket.

"Which way is the Crystal trail?"

He led me out the side door and pointed up the hill.

"Follow this track around the bend in the lake. About a quarter mile beyond the bend it forks and one is marked to Crystal, the left-hand one. As you get up the mountain it forks again, and again it's marked and you take the left. You can't miss it, unless there's much cloud but there doesn't look to be right now, far as you can tell from here what it's liable to be higher up. And I'll tell the inspector soon as he comes in."

"Thanks. You do that."

I hit the trail. I thought for a moment of going to get

the revolver from the car but then I thought I would not use the extra time so I hit the trail instead. I wanted to catch up with Janet before she could catch up with Begg. I thought I had a good chance because I figured that Begg would be making plenty of time in order to get to Sellick before Ives could sight him. If Begg could shoot Sellick before Ives could sight him, then he would be, from his point of view at any rate, in the clear. He could easily work it that he shot Sellick, the murderer, in self-defense or, in the unlikely event that Sellick was unarmed, to prevent him from escaping. Begg would be figuring like that, I was sure. The sort of man who would take the bold chance of that drive in and out of Beverly was the sort of man who would do just that, ignorant as he was of the fact that we had found him out.

Begg would be traveling as fast as he could, probably faster than Janet could travel. But I didn't care to underestimate Janet. She had not taken long to get out of my tie-up. She had not taken long at all. Certainly I had done it in too much of a hurry, but even so it had been pretty good going for a girl to get out of that, and to do it so quickly. She was a determined girl, that Janet. I thought of her face as it was when she was struggling with me and I knew it must be something the same right now, there ahead of me on the trail, as she went hurrying up the mountain, determined to catch up with Begg and "have things out with him." And now that I had put it into her head that he might be Letty's murderer as well as her lover I had put Janet in worse danger than ever. She was perfectly capable of coming right out with it to him if she thought there was anything in it at all. You couldn't stop a girl like that Janet.

I hurried on as fast as I could. The moon had long gone, the moon that we had seen earlier in the evening, such a very long time ago, and it was not at all easy to see one's way along the trail. Even the starlight was not as bright as it normally was for there were low clouds scudding the sky, that is to say the clouds were not low as compared to sea level, but low as compared to my level which was around eight to nine thousand feet already. And the big trees didn't help to light the trail either. The big firs, Douglas firs they were, that grew down to the edge of the lake.

It was cold. It was cold and it was going to get colder the higher we went and the nearer the hour came to the Californian false dawn. I thought of Janet in just that wool jacket and then I started to laugh at myself for worrying about a girl's catching cold when she might be catching a bullet in her heart.

I came to a fork in the trail, and it was unmarked. The little man had not mentioned it. The first one he had mentioned was a quarter of a mile beyond the bend in the lake and I had only just reached the bend in the lake. The little man had forgotten to mention this fork at all. I wondered if he had also forgotten to mention it to Janet or to Begg. Probably he had gotten so bored at having to describe the way three times he had cut it short in my case. I took the left-hand one on principle and hoped for the best. I knew there was a good chance it might just run down to the edge of the lake, and if it did that I would not be too badly off, whereas if I took the right-hand trail I might go very far wrong indeed.

Suddenly I realized a possibility. I realized that if either Begg or Janet had taken the left-hand trail and if also the left-hand trail, which I was now on, did merely run down to the lake, then either Begg or Janet or both of them would have to turn and come back, and, in doing so, might meet each other, or just one of them might meet me. I tightened the grip on my rifle, holding it ready to raise to my shoulder in a flash, and hurried down the trail as fast as I could.

I met nobody. I met nobody at all on the ever-darkening trail, darkening because the big trees were crowding in thicker here than they had been further back, and then, suddenly, I saw an expanse of whiteness ahead of me through the gaps in the trees, and I saw the lake, and I saw

144

that the trail ran into a clearing on the edge of the lake. The clearing was empty. I had to go all the way back to the fork again, cursing the little man under my breath. He had cost me a good twenty minutes. He might have cost a life. In twenty minutes you can go a long way in the right direction. I knew that now I might very well not catch up with them before the dawn light came, and by the dawn light we should all of us be able to see Crystal Lake, high above us at present, and we should be able to see if there were any man fishing the dawn on the lake, or anyone sleeping in his camp around the lake, or if Sellick had already packed in farther to the back country.

I wondered how far behind me was Ives. It was of course just possible that by now he was ahead of me, having passed me when I was on the wrong trail. I did not know how long it would take him to get back from the pack station to the hotel. You would not think it could take twenty minutes. On the other hand I had an idea that I was probably making better time than Ives who was an older man, so that were he just ahead of me, I would soon overtake him, whereas I could gain nothing by waiting in case he were just immediately behind me, which he might well be.

I came to the marked fork, the first one, and took the left trail as the little man had described. This time it started really to climb. Now you really began to feel the effect of the altitude, the thin air and shortening of breath unaccustomed to it. There was no longer any question of speed. The question was how far up one could climb without stopping for breath.

By the time I reached the second fork a long time had passed, and I was a great deal higher up. Already I could begin to see a faint glimmering of light in the eastern portion of the sky, and the line of the mountain across the valley was discernible. The air was now at its coldest, fraught with the advent of new snow.

The trail leveled off considerably after the second fork, in places even going downhill slightly, then climbing again

145

further on. I was beginning to be able to tell the contours of my immediate vicinity now, and I could see that the trail was skirting a high cliff which might well be the southern shelter of Crystal Lake. It looked as though the trail were only waiting for a suitable pass in order to penetrate the cliff since I was now traveling laterally instead of forward as before.

About an hour later I was proved right. The trail turned sharply, following a fold in the cliff wall and mounting steeply over the pass. At the top the elevation must have been very great, it was the highest point that I had reached in the whole journey, and now the real dawn was beginning, the dawn on the high mountains.

I looked down, ahead of me, and there, still in the shadows of the departing night, Crystal Lake lay in its mountain basin. It was not a large lake, but it was certainly very beautiful, perhaps the most beautiful lake that I had ever seen, although, in comparing the respective beauties of lakes or of women or of jewels or of horses, there is always the difference in the beholder's eye.

And then I saw the fisherman.

Chapter Fifteen

HE WAS standing at the head of the lake, rubber-clad, in the water up to his thighs, and even as I first caught sight of him he was making a cast. Although he was perhaps some four to five hundred yards distant from me, and some two hundred feet below, so that I was unable to recognize his features, I could tell by the way in which he moved and by the shape of that familiar figure that it was George Sellick. I looked carefully around the lake to see any other figures which might be visible and then I saw also the figure of a woman wearing slacks and a mountain jacket moving along the trail some halfway along the side of the lake, her hair bouncing up and down as she half ran and half walked along the trail. Yet nowhere could I see Begg Holbrook, nor any other person.

I ran forward down the hill, searching with my eyes as I ran, and still I could not see him. I could see the camp now, with two animals tethered beside the small, lone tent, there on the other side of the lake. And then, even as I was running forward, I heard the sound of a rifle shot.

At once I looked at Sellick to see if he had been hit. I saw the splash of the bullet in the water some three to four feet from him, and I saw him turn to look in the direction whence the shot had come. I heard him shout, and his words came clearly to me over the surface of the water.

"What the devil do you think you're shooting at, you stupid fool?"

There was no answer, but now I could see him, I could see Begg Holbrook, lying there on the bank beside a boulder, and he was taking deliberate aim at his human target some two hundred yards from him. I knew he was bound to score a hit within his next couple of shots, perhaps within his next shot.

I had my rifle at the ready. Throwing myself forward onto the ground, I raised it to my shoulder and took the first pressure on the trigger.

I got him in my sights and fired a fraction of a second before he fired his second shot at Sellick. I saw my bullet spatter up the dirt a good six feet from him, high and to the left.

I looked at Sellick. At first I thought that this time he had been hit. He dropped his fishing rod and was now crouching down in the water. Then I saw what he was doing. He had his left arm crooked before him and he was drawing a revolver with his right and resting it on his left arm as he aimed for a fantastic shot. He was out of efficient revolver range and all that he could hope to do was to put Holbrook off his aim.

My own shot had already partly succeeded in doing that.

147

For a moment Begg Holbrook turned his head to see who was shooting at him. Meanwhile I was taking aim for my second shot, and Janet was there, halfway between us, almost in my line of fire.

Sellick fired and missed. I was afraid for one moment that his speeding revolver bullet might hit Janet but she was still running forward. Just before she reached my own line of fire I drew a deep breath and steadied myself as I have never steadied myself before. I squeezed the trigger, fired.

Begg Holbrook jerked upwards and fell back, dropping his rifle from his hands as he fell back. This time I had not missed. And even as I was getting up to my feet I saw that Janet had reached him and then knelt down beside him. I had only just fired in time.

I heard running footseps behind me and looked up. There was Ives. How he had made it in the time that he did I shall never know, but there he was, breathing heavily, almost in a state of collapse, but there, present and on the job.

He said, "That was pretty fancy shooting, Foraker. But I'm afraid you're not going to get the credit for it. Give me that gun."

"What do you mean?"

"I'm getting the credit for that shot, not you. It's in my line of duty, and not in yours, so we'll hear no more about it."

I shrugged and gave him the gun. I looked to see what the others were doing. Sellick was coming out of the lake, on his way to walk around the bank and find out what had been going on. Janet was still kneeling beside Begg Holbrook who was lying very still. I wondered if he was dead or merely wounded.

We ran forward, Ives and I, Ives carrying the rifle. Janet looked up and saw us as we came towards them. She was looking as though she might collapse at any moment, kneeling there with her arms about her husband. When I

148

looked at him I saw at once that he was dead, I think he must just have died in that instant in her arms.

Ives said, "I'm sorry it had to be this way, Mrs. Holbrook, but I found out that he, that he—"

Janet finished the sentence for him.

"I know," she said. "He just told me before he died."

Then she pitched forward on her face. I jumped to her and took her in my arms. She had fainted dead away.

Ives said, "Look after her while I go on and meet him."

I nodded, and he went off to meet Sellick, but I didn't pay any attention to him, I was too busy trying to see what I could do for her. I took off my flight jacket and put it around her. Her hands were like ice and this time I had no brandy or anything. I began rubbing her hands and her feet, her feet were badly bruised and her shoes were in a bad state, they had not been made for the kind of wear they had just been receiving. The sunlight was beginning to reach down over the hill to the lake now, and I knew that shortly she would be in the sunlight.

When Ives and Sellick came she was still away. I looked up at George Sellick. He still looked very much the same as he used to in the olden days, except that now he was older. He gave me a wan smile and said, "Hullo, Foraker, Ives has been telling me."

I smiled at him and said, "Hullo, George. Have you any brandy?"

He was looking down at Janet's face and I saw the little tensing of his facial muscles as he looked at her. He took a flask from the deep pocket of his fishing coat and handed it to me and said, still looking at Janet's face, "I would never have believed it, I would never have believed it. Letty had told me about her, of course, but—"

He gave a little shrug as he handed me the flask and looked at me and then he said, "I think I'll leave this with you. Let's call it a farewell offering, shall we? I don't think I want to be here when she—"

I took the brandy flask from him and I said, "I understand."

He said, "Maybe I should never have asked you for that necklace. I think perhaps every man has to use his own necklace." He held out his hand and I took it. He said, "So long, Foraker, I've got a lot of fishing to do."

I said, "So long, George."

He turned on his heel and walked back along the bank of the lake, back along the way he had come.

I opened the brandy flask and poured out a little of the brandy into the top of the flask and tipped it gently against her lips as she lay there with her head in my arms. I knew that soon now, at any moment, perhaps at the same moment as the sunlight reached us, she would open her eyes and look at me and come alive again.